I AM HOOLIGAN

Emma L. Flint

Publisher Information

I Am Hooligan
Published in 2016 by
Acorn Books
www.acornbooks.co.uk
an imprint of
Andrews UK Limited
www.andrewsuk.com

Novelisation by Emma L. Flint

Based on the film by Steven M. Smith & Chris Bell

*Based on the story and screenplay by Chris Bell,
Steven M. Smith & Christopher Jolley*

Contents

I AM HOOLIGAN

Prologue

Ruffled turned up corners fluttered as a light breeze danced through the open window, the soft flicker laced with the interlocked, diluted smells of the estate, their everyday lives continuing on as normal while he lay there on his bed, staring blankly at the ceiling, lost in a whirl of thoughts that stoked deep emotions like a stick prods at a growing fire. One slip and the stick is engulfed, the flames reaching twisted highs, their dancing colours licking at untouched wood. As the delicate sound of the poster crinkling reached his ears, he turned his attention toward his bedroom wall, adorned with sporting idols and action packed blockbusters, the protagonists eyes gazing back at him, the blankness of their stare as unnerving as they were hypnotising.

The sudden rush of magazine papers flying open on his desk caused him to look longingly towards the window, the gush of wind almost tempting him to escape from the confines of his home, to avoid the dull noises that echoed from downstairs. A deep, lingering sigh heaved his chest high as he averted his eyes back to the ceiling, the peeling paint and cracks rather more interesting than the unpleasantness unfolding below. Despite the cool, seemingly powerful exterior of his bedroom door, the barrier between his world and theirs did little to mute the shouts of fury as his father raged at his mother. *Tuesday... it must be fucking Tuesday... he only really goes for it on a Tuesday.* Justin wasn't sure what was worse at this point: having to listen to the frantic vocals of his dad, or the fact that he could tell the day of the week by his dad's behaviour.

Disheartened and uncomforted by either, he returned to his thoughts, his mind now seething, the rush of anger building in him; while no match for his father's it still had a fury all of its own. As the momentum built so too did the tension in his body, turning him into a fidgeting mess as he tried to shift to a more comfortable position. The bed felt like lead, it had no softness or warmth, it was a flat slab further agitating him. *I can't remember a time when he was nice. I can't ever remember a time when anything was nice.* His jaw throbbed at the pain of being incessantly clenched, the force of his grinding teeth vibrating deep inside his head, mixing in with the increasing argument. *Life is hard. I'm not complaining, I'm not the sort to complain. But if you want to know the sort of person I am, you've only got to look at who my fucking Dad is.* The raising beat of his heart floods his ears, yet another niggling sound adding to the oncoming crescendo. *Always starts with the fucking Dad.*

WHACK! The torturous sound of skin colliding with skin snapped him violently from his inner turmoil. A momentary silence hung in the air, the lack of anything somewhat more painful than the sound of the hit itself. And there it was, his mother starting to cry as the realisation of another beating sunk in as she nursed her red welt of bruised skin. Instincts coursing through his veins, Justin leapt up off of his bed, his feet landing with a light thud on the carpeted floor. But then he froze – what was he actually going to do if he went downstairs and confronted them? Even though the intention of good was there, he knew it would cause more harm in the end, and then there was the painful truth that he didn't *want* to get involved. It wasn't that he didn't want to help his mother, he did more than anything, but it was more the fact that he didn't want to be near his dad. He didn't want his dirty temper to touch and taint him.

Calmly, clinically, he stepped away from the foreboding leer of his door and walked towards his beaten up but trusty stereo;

he needed the hum of music, the deafening sounds of safety that would keep him sane through the darkest storms. Without even a thought to whether his parents would appreciate the sudden appearance of pounding music, he cranked up the volume, only the grip he had on the dial revealing the tension still charging through him. Stood in front of the intrusive abuse of the drop bass and the crashing of drums, Justin remained still, a solitary island inside his personal fortress and allowed the sounds to wash over him, enveloping him in a cocoon that drowned out everything else. A pleasant way to drown. Finally, when he regained a little bit of self awareness, he wandered over to his bed and threw himself down hard, the mattress giving only a little upon impact.

Chapter One

*I*t was a battlefield of incomparable violence, an unrelenting force driven by the most malicious intent, fuelled by alcohol and a deeply misguided sense of defending what was theirs. It was their family, their life. Something that precious deserved to be protected at all costs, and against any who dared to say otherwise. There was no fear, no hesitation, just the need to hurt. To crush and break. One well placed punch, a kick, a broken bottle – their arsenal was whatever was to hand, a deadly combination of innovation that was as frightening as impressive. It was a fantastic display, but for all the wrong reasons; humanity was dead here in this chaotic sea of faceless hooligans.

Oh, it was a war, but not the ones fought over gods and kings but over a popular pastime. Football. In some ways a lot more of a damning religion than any others found in the world, for the passion it fuelled burnt as bright as the sun and stung deep in your muscles, red hot pokers driving you to act. Although no physical shots were fired, the hurling spittle and drops of blood gave the effect of a massacre having taken place. What a sorrowful sight to behold, and there was no letting up. They would consume everything in their path, for how dare anyone stop their love of their sport.

A flash of curled up digits rushed towards the blurred vision of an angry participant, his senses barely registering what was coming his way before the fist and the assailant fell away and the world turned to black.

The horrors of football warfare, while encompassing a wide area, hadn't managed to reach here. Here was tranquil, peaceful and free, the silence interrupted only by the tweets of birds and the odd purr of a car driving in the near distance. It was quite beautiful in its own way. Justin scanned the ground, his eyes moving over the course, enjoying the lack of presence save for himself and his friend, Eddie. Anyone watching would simply see a couple of dots in the distance roaming the green, the entire golf course for them and them alone on this day. He breathed in a lungful of fresh air, a slight sting prickling along his throat as the freshness whipped the sensitive flesh there.

A clear of a throat from beside him brought Justin back to the here and now, and the ball planted by his feet awaiting to be projected through the air to its far flung destination. In a relatively fluid motion, the club hit the ball squarely on the side and sent it flying skyward, whizzing through the air at great speed. As he watched it go, Justin was silently thankful for the lack of people at the course today.

"Not bad." Eddie cut in, ensuring that his friend stayed humble in the face of victory at having successfully landed a good hit. Unimpressed by the lack of feeling behind his so called compliment, Justin turned to look at him, a raised eyebrow slightly crinkling his brow.

"Not bad? I just sent that fucking ball to Mars!" As if it would amplify his point, Justin stretched his arm out behind him, pointing at the empty air, the ball that had recently rocketed across the green having landed. Eddie gave a shrug, but a sly smile started to cross his face, a low joyful laugh rolling off his tongue.

"Yeah… but it beats you taking chunks out of the green."

Rolling his eyes up towards the sky, he stepped aside to let Eddie take position ready for his next shot. With his back now to him, Justin quietly muttered "Such a smart arse." as he watched his friend line up his body and practised a few swings. Even though he couldn't see it, he knew that the other boy was wearing a big grin as he heard the mumbled words "That's me." in response as he finalised the line up of the ball on the tee, concentration etched on his features. "So what you up to this weekend?"

Titling his head to one side, mimicking a dog hard of hearing, Justin responded nonchalantly, as if it was already obvious what his plans were – "I was going to see Kevin." Nothing. Silence between the two as Eddie proceeded to fiddle about with the ball, as if he was finely tuning a vast machine rather than positioning a golf ball. Under normal circumstances Justin wouldn't have minded the silence between them for it was never awkward, sadly though, on this occasion it was and he knew exactly why. "What?"

"I didn't say anything."

"No… you didn't have to. Come on, what's your problem with him?"

That slight pause again, just as the silence of the other day had been overwhelming when his parents had been fighting, so too was this. In fact in some ways it was worse because he couldn't fathom for the life of him why Eddie had such an issue with Kevin. It wasn't that he expected his friend to like everyone he did, he wasn't that unrealistic about the world, but it just seemed so unusual for him to dislike someone in this way. And try as he might to not let it bother him, he couldn't help but be annoyed and confused. Eddie turned toward the other, completely disregarding the ball he had so tediously moved about on top of the tee, his eyes soft but full of… worry? Justin wasn't too sure what emotion was reaching out to him. More of the soundless void dragging between them, the very air laced with it; giving in, reluctantly, he threw a cutting remark his way "I suppose you're perfect." It wasn't a question, it was a sarcastic statement designed to provoke a response.

"No… nobody's perfect. Look, I don't mind you hanging out with Kevin, just, well, just be careful yeah?"

Although annoyance still laced his actions, Justin couldn't help soften slightly; this was his friend here, and someone who had a few more years of experience on top of him. Having gotten out of a pretty rough lifestyle previously, Eddie had managed to clean up his life and integrate into normal society, so it made sense that he was worried about Kevin for he embodied the opposite. That being said, Justin couldn't understand why there was so much concern surrounding this one person – association didn't naturally lead to becoming the same, not as far as he was concerned, so it felt that Eddie was wasting his time ultimately. To comply, albeit it begrudgingly, Justin simply nodded his head and let that brief action be symbol enough, an aspect that didn't sit right with Eddie. "Justin?" It was one word, his name, nothing more, but the whole tone and phrasing of those six letters infuriated him no end.

"You're not my dad, Eddie. Drop it." No pleasantries now, no please and thank yous, this was his way of defending his right to be his own person. Screw the fact he was only 18, he knew the world, he'd had a rough enough time with his father to know what was what and that life wasn't all roses and sunshine, he didn't need the point ramming down his throat. He heard a gentle sigh as Eddie looked his way.

"Just be careful."

Again, it was that sincerity that stung harshest of all, for Justin knew it was all meant well, even if the delivery wasn't nicely packaged. Not that that would make him let his friend off, oh no, there was a time and place to talk about such things and this wasn't it. All he'd wanted was to enjoy some peace and quiet away from his drunkard father who would doubtedly be stumbling about bellowing at the top of his lungs. But instead he got landed with a spot of golf that had now turned into some life critique. He hoped that would be the end of it, but Eddie's eyes continued to burn into the side of Justin's face, the younger of the two trying desperately to ignore the eyes he could see blazing with such intensity. It was maddening, and soon became too much for him to handle. "Are you going to take this shot then or not?" In reality he didn't care whether the shot was taken or not, hell, sod the ball and sod the golf course, but he just wanted to say something to defuse this tension between them.

"Alright… alright…" His companion mumbled while he finally moved his eyes off of Justin and back onto the ball, the inanimate object looking almost pleased to be noticed once again.

Chapter Two

Desolation was what this part of the neighbourhood offered to those who dare venture, and of those people there were but a few. It was exactly like a scene from *Shameless*, burnt out cars and screaming kids claiming the scrap as their castle lined virtually every street. The only problem was, this wasn't some fictional estate that brought laughs more than sorrow, it was the real hard hitting world, an unkind creature that shaped you far more than any public school education and money ever could. Although it would harden you, train you to face the more painful elements of life, it did so in a way that chipped a little of your soul away each time. Justin winced a little as he tried to ignore the scenery before him. Despite being his home it wasn't a place he was fond of, and neither were the authorities. Oh no, they hated this place much more than he did for they knew what lurked there and would rather leave the 'rabble' to deal with their own lives and stick to more refined lifestyles. That was how it felt to him, and as far as he was concerned he was right.

Distracting as the landscape was, with a stereo now pumping out such heavy music that the whole street nearly quaked, it was nothing compared to Kevin rambling on beside him. His mouth was like a motor, and it was in overdrive as he told Justin about all the juicy drama that had gone down at the weekend; by the sounds of things it had been mental. And messy. "it proper went off at the fucking weekend, mate!" That little spatter of information computed over everything else and made Justin prick his ears up to hear all the bloody details.

"What happened?" Kevin didn't need this prod to tell a story, he'd just do it anyway and expect you to listen, but Justin wanted to appear eager, and in some respects he really was. His friend's stories always sounded so exhilarating. A grin lined the slightly older but no wiser face of his 23 year old friend, a look of delight dancing there.

"It was the play off, mate and a rival fucking firm wanted to have it. Fuck that! We fucking smashed them up, mate, good and fucking proper," Justin wasn't sure whether more fucks and fuckings could be added to a sentence, but Kevin's foul mouth always had a surprise in store for him. "There was this one guy, a massive fuck off cunt, and he wanted it thinking he was some kind of hard nut. Ha! I had this fucking beer bottle – you know the ones? Anyway, I took it and smashed it right across his fucking face. Bang! Right fucking there." As a means of demonstration, as if one was needed after such a colourful retelling, Kevin ran a finger across his face. "He was pissing blood like a proper fucking cunt. Started crying like one too." His finishing words morphing into a deep, sinister laugh as he played the images through his head. Kevin was revelling in the destruction of it all, the chaos a firm partner in crime for him.

He was probably expecting Justin to ask some fangirl like questions demanding more details, wanting the gore, but instead the teenager innocently asked what the end score had been. To Justin, it made sense that you would only cause that level of insanity if there was a good enough reason behind it – why start a huge fight if there was no need? This level of logic though didn't appear to inhabit Kevin's natural thought processes, judging by his response.

"What?"

Still rather innocently, Justin persisted "What was the score in the end?"

"How the fuck should I know?"

Although he remained blank on the outside, inside he was pretty confused as to how Kevin couldn't know this information. Not that he was about to keep asking, he didn't want to upset his friend, and not just because the friendship would be at risk. There was no denying that Kevin had an air about him that struck fear into many, nor could you ignore how he swaggered around the estate like a proud peacock, lording over everyone. Quite simply, even if they weren't friends, this guy wasn't someone you wanted to unnecessarily piss off. "I played golf." He wasn't sure why he went with that as his opening, but he had done it now so there was no going back.

"What? Don't tell me it was with that fucking homo Eddie?" He responded, distain coating his features. There was obviously no love lost between Eddie and Kevin, but it wasn't like either one had done something to the other, so it seemed like an unnecessary hatred. Dislike more on Eddie's part, he was too gentle nowadays to project hate out into the world, whereas hatred was exactly what Kevin felt for the other man, and a lot of it too. Feeling the need to stick up for Eddie, much like he would for Justin, he stated matter of factly that Eddie was in no shape or form a homo, much to the annoyance of Kevin. "Yes he fucking is – he plays golf all the time? Fucking queer." There was just no defending Eddie in this little bubble that Kevin and Justin inhabited as they walked through the bruised and battered streets of their estate. The cocoon they created around themselves, impervious to outside harm, was more Kevin's than Justin's, as the older of the two dominated their personal space much like he did everything else. In some ways you could describe his command over the world as majestic, but it was a twisted kind of regality that was as frightening as it was awe-inspiring.

Sensing that the question (or lack of) of Eddie's sexuality would keep rearing its ugly head unless he changed the subject, Justin tried to divert the conversation back to Kevin's brawling. Not only could he then show off his hardman persona, but it meant Justin could hear more about the fight, something which although he would never admit openly, he secretly wanted to know. He wasn't a violent person by any means, but he couldn't let that kind of story pass him by. "As if you really had a barney with a rival firm." *Nothing like stoking the flames there, Justin. Live dangerously and all that.*

"Are you saying I'm fucking lying?!"

"Come on, Kevin, you haven't got a fucking mark on you." He snorted back, amused at how readily his mate rose to the occasion, it was predictable but funny, and he knew that there was no real danger. It was two lads having some banter, nothing more, and the use of similar language to his friend just helped solidify that fact.

"It's because I was fucking lucky – you best not be saying I'm fucking lying!"

"Oh, piss off! Besides, I'm safe here, there's no bottles lying around."

An explosion of laughter ignited between them as they amused themselves with the violent intricacies of the weekend fight, the fact that it was very real and had caused serious harm forgotten on both of them. *This* is why Justin enjoys Kevin's company so much: for the laughter and fun he brings. Sure he has a 'bad side', but so does everyone, and a lot of the time Justin is in no danger of the other's rage for he's a partner in crime in Kevin's eyes, another disciple to bring into the fold. And that group didn't seem so bad when Justin looked at it completely objectively, without Eddie sounding in his subconscious; they did cause pockets of trouble, but the conductor of this lethal orchestra, the one next to him, he couldn't be all bad could he? After all, he had all these people surrounding him, following him.

Breathlessly, the laughter stinging his throat and burning the muscles in his cheeks, Kevin finally broke the voidless vacuum of laughter. "Seriously though, mate, you want to be spending time with me." He paused to suck in a huge lungful of air, a desperate attempt to keep the giggles in check. "My whole life is brawling, crawling, drinking, drugging, and women." The very last word was music to Justin's ears, and would undoubtedly be so of many 18 year old boys; women, their sexual prowess and beauty could turn heads, unleash unbridled passion, and cause you the most awkward of discomforts when your joggers became a little too tight. He was fine without the fighting and all its trimmings – they sounded fun but they didn't *move* him.

"That sounds alright…" He didn't know how else to play it: come in strong and sound like a child clutching to be accepted by his role model, or sound too indifferent and have disappointment stare back at you blankly. Neither was the outcome he wanted, so he kept it cool and casual, for it seemed to be the wisest move to make. Kevin, however, didn't seem impressed with his blasé mumble. He'd wanted eagerness, excitement spilling out of Justin's eyes as he looked upon someone who had the key to Disneyland and had just offered to share it. But instead he got 'alright'. Suitable, agreeable, fucking satisfactory wasn't what he cared for or wanted to hear.

"Alright? Just alright?! It's better than fucking alright! Mate, if you want to be part of this world, going through the usual bollocking nine to five grind, then there has to be something to work for."

"What do you work for?" Complete innocence framed in a five word sentence, presented to a man who couldn't give a shit.

"The weekend. I work for the *weekend*. I fucking *live* for the weekend. It's all you can do."

W-e-e-k-e-n-d. It had been said in such quick succession that Justin couldn't help but muse at how odd it sounded now. And how mythical. The religious love Kevin had for the weekend, that drive to work for nothing but those two days, made the whole thing resonate with him on a deeper level. Although there was depth there, and something about that word clung to his brain and demanded he be engulfed by its so called prolific qualities, he still felt unsure. Living for two days out of seven felt... wasted, as if Kevin was discarding important time that nobody truly had because the sand pouring into the hourglass never played fair. His expression matched his inner turmoil: lines crinkled as he frowned, his eyes searching for something that made everything rushing from Kevin's mouth appear worthwhile. Kevin, however, allowed a Cheshire Cat grin to spread across his cocoa coloured skin, its sudden appearance and growing width making it as unnerving as being greeted by the talking cat himself. "You know what? You should come out with me tonight."

An invite? Now was his chance to step over that threshold of casual acquaintance to one of the lads, but what to do... "Where?" It was all he had right now, for his mind cascaded with dos and don'ts, a stereotypical angel/devil moment of whether he should or shouldn't go, Eddie's soft but firm warning sounding in the recesses of his mind. The response of it being just a few drinks made it sound so lighthearted, so meaningless and unimportant, and yet he felt turning down the offer wasn't an option. "I don't know..." Further uncertainty hanging in the air between them, growing stale and stagnating a turbulent friendship on the edge of something greater or terribly worse. Still, Kevin persisted on as relentless as ever.

"C'mon, you'll get to meet the crew – they're a good bunch. A good bunch of fucking wankers. Wankers." At risk of making that too sound as god like as 'weekend' had before, maybe it was something to do with words beginning with w? "But they're a good bunch of wankers." Not something Shakespeare would finish with, but it was poetic all the same, albeit dry and unfeeling like dead wood.

Putting aside the argument he was conducting in his head, Justin couldn't help be worried about being ID'd. Embarrassing didn't quite convey the evil of this social suicide. "If I'm asked for ID I'll look a right fucking cunt."

"They won't – they're so desperate for fucking punters they'll serve anyone."

"You sure?"

"Of course I'm fucking sure! So, are you up for it?"

***

Although the question continued to probe him, the decision had been made and decided upon, which is why his bedroom is currently in complete disarray as he tries to find appropriate clothes. No doubt many can look back at the time and effort they poured into getting ready for a night out and smile, blaming adolescence for their need to be 'perfect', but Justin hadn't had that hindsight luxury. Something that is highly amusing to the teenage girl sat crossed leg like a yoga goer on his bed, mindlessly flicking through the pages of a dirty mag, her eyes twitching over at photograph that assaults them. Justin couldn't help but grin absentmindedly as he watched Danielle continue to be quietly offended by the girls spreading their all to a world of normally very engaged clientele.

Why she had wanted to come hang when he'd insisted, quite adamantly, that he had to get ready he had no idea, but her company was sort of welcome now it was here. She was a normal constant in his life, and had been for many years, and she managed to hold niggling doubts at bay even though she had no idea that was her superpower at all. Not that he would even consider telling her – she'd love to know she had such a profound affect on him. "Do you actually read these, or do you just spend your time wanking over them?" Cut across the room with a genuine tinge of curiosity lacing its otherwise sarcastic attack.

"Dani, seriously? For fuck sake!" He replied with a mock sense of dismay colouring his features, his inability to stifle his laughter destroying the whole image. Memories of them as children playing and giggling about a world they didn't understand now transformed into Danielle asking about wanking; it wasn't right, but it made him happy.

Persisting, as always, she allowed another question to fall between them, only this time there was a more serious undertone. "How do you expect women to measure up to this?" Glancing over at the page she was exposing, a two page spread (so aptly named) of a beautifully toned stunner draped over a bed, her legs wide open to draw the eye to her most intimate of places. There was a slight artistic flare lurking amongst the details, but it was mainly a means of shoving a lot of tits and pussy into the reader's faces and allowing them to imagine being able to savour every inch of that view first hand. It was completely unrealistic, hence its erotic charm, not to mention he could sound off about how men were meant to live up to the likes of buffed up men in all the films Dani swooned over, but he decided not to. He was busy. Night out and all that.

"I don't want them to measure up."

"No wonder we didn't last."

Her matter of fact face, coupled with that assute if misguided conclusion, made Justin howl the room down, his laughter unforgiving to all ears within his immediate vicinity; Danielle was too much fun! "We were boyfriend and girlfriend in primary school!"

"Yes, and I was heartbroken."

"You're nuts."

Their back and forth could go on like a snooker championship, so readily did they have jibes and jabs to sling at the other, but now wasn't the right time for the clock was counting down and Justin still needed to finish getting ready.

Popping the top off his aftershave with ease, Justin doused himself in the fragrance, the light spray flying towards clean clothes and masking it with their scent; a mindless, uncontrolled invasion of every fibre of material. And evidently an attack on Danielle who started to cough and splutter as the aroma began to fly about the room. The density was thickening, like fog, a hazy blanket over her eyes, shrouding Justin in a toxic cloud of overpriced cologne. "Bloody hell!" She managed to stammer between coughs, the tiny particles joyeously tickling along her throat and pushing up her nostrils.

"What?" Justin implored, feigned care in his voice; he knew exactly what the problem was and was revelling in her spewing up the contents of his aftershave.

"You know damn well what," A little more heated than he'd expected, the fine balance between humour and annoyance completely at a loss of where to redraw the line. "Is your plan to knock out anyone with that smell of that stuff if they try to ID you?" And the humour had won out, for now.

As if deciding it was safe for him to push his luck that little further, he pressed down firmly on the release once more, a fresh plume of scent springing into the air, their end goal now everything and anything in their line of sight. Danielle looked on in shock stained awe, unsure whether she was impressed by his cheek, or whether she wanted to ram the canister down his neck until he choked on it. "Ha ha. Very fucking funny." Justin shouted as the artificial rain tumbled down and coated them both.

"I don't want to sound like Eddie, but…" It slipped from her mouth so suddenly Justin had to repeat the words inside his head once more; what had just been a happy scene of bickering and laughter had now turned into a serious tomb for them both to occupy. Inwardly he sighed, for he didn't want to get into this again. *He* wanted to go out, have a few drinks, make a few new friends, then come home and sleep. There was no master plan to turn into Kevin, and certainly no incentive for him to become that which he feared: his dad, so why did Danielle feel the need to rain on his parade just as Eddie had done?

Justin knew they both meant well, they were his friends and they looked out for him as much as they did themselves, but he so wished they changed the record and mention a fresh warning every now and again. They were making Kevin the boogeyman, not Kevin himself. "I know what you're going to say." *So don't. Not now, don't ruin it, Dani.*

"Kevin's bad news, Justin. It's only a matter of time before he gets himself killed, or worse, someone else."

"He's not that bad, he just likes a rumble every now and again, that's all." If the words were ringing hollow to him then he was sure they did to Danielle, but he had no idea what else he could say to her.

"You could do something else?" Dani suggested, the higher pitch tone of the end signalling that she was throwing all her hope onto this last minute train. Justin felt he couldn't win – if he cancelled now, not only would he look a royal twat, but he'd also lose respect of someone who you didn't want to mess with, but on the reverse if he did go out he had to deal with Dani's suffocating disappointment.

Finally braving the silence that sounded like an air horn, Justin was about to ask the very real question of what it was she actually expected him to do instead, as if staying in was an option for him. Right on cue, as if some divine interventions had decided fate for him, a loud slam of the front door, followed by animated shouting flying up to the other side of his bedroom door to greet both himself and Danielle. The bellows of fury grow louder and reached the climax of an almighty slap, leaving the question answered as far as Justin was concerned, a fact that Danielle seemed to accept without interfering further. She had heard this scene play out before, and she knew how much it broke Justin when he couldn't escape from it, a prisoner to his own family of dysfunction. Kevin was no better, in fact he was worse as far as she was concerned, however, he wasn't the one cornering Justin's mum right now and beating her like a dusty rug against a wall.

The rest of their brief time together was immersed in interrupted silence, the thwack of skin and the ceaseless moans from downstairs an exclusive show that neither of them wanted a part of.

Chapter Three

H is journey to the pub was one of mixed emotions, an internal battle of whether he should have remained at home to meekly protect his mother, or whether he was doing the right thing getting in deeper with Kevin. As he had waved Danielle goodbye she had looked at him with searching eyes brimming with the need to be noticed, to be heeded; it had unnerved him. They had had disagreements in the past, some of which had been due to who was hanging around with who, but this was different. The streets that they called home had crafted them into the stereotypical chavs in the papers; trackies and gold hoops, disruption and the people to cross the streets from, but that didn't mean they were without awareness of who was truly bad and who just played at it. Estates across the UK had plenty of fools placing themselves at the head of some dysfunctional street gang, whose ambitions amounted to smacking some spray paint on the local supermarket and then running. And even when they did experiment with violence, it never snowballed out of control: there was a flash of a knife, a weak threat, and then everyone scattered like rats as the police rolled up with their eagerly awaiting handcuffs. Kevin and his guys were different. Justin knew it and so did Dani, the only difference was that she felt a greater threat emanating from Kevin while Justin simply envisioned him as another wannabe. There was potential there to evolve into one of those council estate monsters that scare the middle and upper classes into wanting to keep the poverty stricken down, but he doubted that Kevin would fully commit.

Wrapped up so deeply in the blankets of tumbling questions, Justin almost forgot the door raising up in front of him, his face stopping inches before colliding with the dingy glass and wood. A rattling sigh betrayed him as he eyed the buildings exterior cautiously; this was it, the border between nations, the place where he could become more than a boy and yet was at obvious risk of becoming a symbol of shame. Lightly his hand pushed against the sticky grain and applied pressure, a world of new smells rushing at him in frenzied excitement.

Despite the fact that it was a weeknight, the pub was heaving like the struggling chest of a heavy smoker, everyone held within the rise and fall of the beat and the laughs of drunken joy. In the face of his cynicism and caution, he did allow himself to marvel at how drink brought together people of all ages, as if numbers had no place here, just relaxation and good cheer. For Justin, a boy so used to scornful looks that they don't cause him upset anymore, it was nice to see the older generation accepting that the younger could do things other than cuss and make trouble. As his eyes roamed over each face, taking in the creases of each set of features, the crinkle at the corners of eyes, the laughter lines, and the puckered lips of smokers, he finally found a waving hand. Hidden away in a corner sat Kevin and his friends, a broad grin, no sneer, adorning Kevin's face. He knew he had Justin in his grasps now. "There he is!" He boomed over the noise, the heads surrounding him now turning in unison to look at their new friend – *their new victim.*

Settling himself firmly beside Kevin, a clear and new favourite for the others to glare at and then grin with acceptance, Justin smiled appropriately as he gave a friendly 'hello' to his mates. The brave smile that clung to his youthful face didn't fool the other, for he knew all too well how daunting Justin was finding this new world, a place where he was nothing and Kevin was king.

"Don't look so fucking scared, you look like a rabbit caught in headlights." The amusement peppered his voice, and while it made Justin feel like a child playing grown up, he couldn't help but feel accepted when Kevin pulled him into a one arm hug and waved a hand to the group. "Let me introduce you to the crew." Four men were now presented to him, their expressions expectant, waiting for the boy to either mess up or become one of them. One man was quickly signalled out. "This is Milton."

The one named Milton eyed Justin with bubbling amusement coming off of him in waves; he was obviously entertained by Justin in some way, and the teenager felt he knew why. *Here it comes, Justin…*

"Fucking hell, Kevin, did he escape from a nursery?" And there it was, the jibe about his age. In a place where numbers didn't matter to the rest of the patrons, here it mattered most. Chuckles circulated the group, but Justin remained stony, attempting to be unmoved by the childish comments.

"Have the old people's home let you out for day release?" His quick wit and equally cheeky remark heralded a bigger, healthier reception from everyone there, Milton included; he'd successfully passed his first test. Although the roars still ripped through the small group, Kevin was already moving on to single out another of his flock, a man who looked to be of a similar age to Milton. It amazed Justin how older men were so willing to follow someone younger than them, or maybe they didn't picture Kevin the same way he did.

"This is Frankie, though his real name is Franz." *French, cool,* Justin mused, looking this new acquaintance up and down, taking him all in and making mental images. Even though he didn't want to rely upon the archetypes of French features, he couldn't help but inwardly smile at how French Frankie was: the firm jaw, the dark hair, the slimy yet overtly friendly, somewhat obnoxious expression. A thick accent, worn a little by the culture of Britain but still able to stand its ground, started to ring in Justin's ears; a rough jar against the hum of the pub.

"We stick to Frankie because these reprobates can't handle my accent."

22

"You're French?" He needlessly enquired, knowing full well what answer he was about to receive.

"I am. I've been travelling through Europe and got stuck here, and haven't left in a year." Now it was time for Kevin to pipe up, eager to bring the control back to his reigns and his alone.

"Don't worry, once the World Cup comes round Frankie's going to be fucking off home."

As if right on cue the group erupted into fits of giggles, mimicking schoolgirls more than grown men, although their childish antics were lost on the room for they were all too busy focusing on their own laughter. The trickling, the booming, the harsh with the light came together to create an eclectic band of amusement that was pleasant to the ears. Outsiders would hear it as a beacon to partake in the fun, while those in the room used it as confirmation that being there despite it being a work night was a wise decision. Their gaggle of sound was soon turned down when Kevin moved along to his next member, a gentleman sat next to Frankie who oozed so much confidence it was stifling. "Frankie's mate here, George, he's even fucking worse." Justin didn't have to wait long to find out why, for before he could ask George muscled in, grabbed his hand and did enough talking for everyone in the room.

"George. And no, I'm not a foreigner, I'm as English as they come." As if following a plot they all knew perfectly well, Frankie now seized the limelight and continued on with the story.

"I met George when he was travelling through Paris." His lilt added exoticism to each word, making it all the more interesting and exciting to Justin, who so far in his life had seen the full extent of his estate and the town it resided in. Of course, he was coloured impressed in every sense of the word, but he didn't want that to come across too strongly to those now ogling him as he sat and nodded like a bobblehead. All he could manage was a smile, while systematically thinking *fucking hell*, followed by listening to George's sudden admission-

23

"I like fucking and fighting." *It seems everyone does here... Not bad though, sounds fun,* Justin mused as he watched Kevin crease into laughter once more.

Finally he was introduced to the last member of this ragtag band of merry men, and this particular gentleman had a more formal air about him; he rose up and swiftly shook Justin's hand, eyeing the boy with sharpened interest, a cat watching its prey. "Lloyd." Straight to the point, no messing, no fuss, and definitely no chorus of the mantra of fucking and fighting which all these lads apparently enjoyed doing more than living. It amazed Justin in several ways, many of which all conversed at one main point of awe: these men, however untamed and wild, they had the keys to a pastime like no other. They promised a world of excitement that Justin had craved for so long, desperate to avoid the deafening smacks and wails of his father and mother. And here it was, laid before him, all he had to do was defy friends advice and plunge head first into unknown waters.

Realising that he had been quiet a little too long, especially given the fact that someone had just introduced themselves, Justin gave a flash of a forced smile and replied "Hello, mate." It was casual, just like him.

"Take a seat, Justin." Milton interjected, his manner light and airy, unlike the stifling warmth of the pub they all inhabited. Obediently, and maybe a little too fast, Justin sat himself down and faced the curved wall of eyes that now blazed at him. They were all friendly enough, and right now Justin was a potential one of them, no threat, and yet those expectant engaged looks made the boy shift in his seat uncomfortably. Being centre stage to a show you weren't sure about in the first place was his idea of hell. Not that he'd walk away now, for it was too late for that, no, he had to endure and firmly become part of the group.

It was Lloyd who broke first. "So then, Justin, what do you do with yourself these days?" Had the atmosphere just spiked a little? Justin felt sure that question had a lot more punch than it appeared to, and he was positive that his answer had the power to terminate his inclusion in this poor man's rendition of King Arthur's Round Table. While he didn't doubt what he thought, he didn't wish to come out with lies of such grandeur that they would laugh him out the door and all the way into his bedroom; honesty was what was needed here.

"Not much, just chilling really."

"Justin's from the same estate as me," Started Kevin, ensuring his precious catch didn't flounder. "It's a right fucking dive, I can tell you."

"It's only you that makes it rough." Added Milton, a twinkle in his eyes that caught fire with Kevin's, more copious amounts of laughter rapping on the doors of throats demanding to be released. Laughter was a currency here, and a telltale sign of being one of the group: no laughter, no entry. They were password protected by deception, for you could search and search and never find the correct phrase because it was all about what the word sounded like when exchanged.

"Fuck off, you cunt." Booming throaty chuckles throwing themselves up into the air, echoing and bouncing in their playful annoyance.

Next up was Frankie. It was like they were doing the rounds of a well rehearsed script: Lloyd would lead, Kevin would explain, and Milton would come in last with a playful jibe that left a climatic opening for Kevin to size, and then the hysterics began. The roles would then be reversed and someone else would take up the mantel Lloyd had championed only moments ago, and the play would start up again. "Been here before?" His lilt caressed, leaving Justin feeling the need to examine whether he'd changed sex within the last few minutes. 'Been here before' sounded a lot like 'come here often' – were they teasing or being serious?

"Right before Frankie asks that he tries to slip his cock in you." Kevin purred, the broken giggles turning him into a cat. Right on cue, everyone applauded with the sounds of their laughter, only this time it soared to new heights, their volume booming louder than everyone else's. It was then that a nearby patron who had been savouring good conversion with his friends, turned and stared at them, a look of disdain painted on his snobbish features.

He was a pointed little man, someone who lacked importance but who clearly felt that accusing stares and passive aggression would cement his place in life; Justin disliked him immediately. This nobody being somebody was so like those who said that his estates, and the likes of him, were scum that sponged and fiddled systems, good-for-nothing's who took advantage of the purity of others. Laughable really, as Justin had come to the conclusion that the rats crowding the streets of Britain were normally the ones pointing fingers at everyone else. This man to his side was a rat.

Although they had all laughed and been lively, the gaze of this particular bystander hadn't gone unnoticed by Milton, he just like Justin had determined that this other wasn't worthy. "What are you looking at you fucking twat?!" Venom spewed from his mouth far quicker than the laughter had earlier, and it shocked Justin somewhat; he didn't like the other man either, but that immediate eruption of abuse seemed uncalled for given that all they had given the group was a look. Surprisingly though, the rat held his nerve, much to Milton's anger. "Fucking prick!" He shouted over, louder than his last comment, inciting his friends into howling once more, only this time it sounded like threatening war cries. The tension was only broken for Justin when Kevin ruffled his hair playfully, an attempt at demonstrating they were having fun, nothing bad was happening, yet the teenager wasn't assured.

Although looks of disdain had followed them around for the entirety of the night, it didn't deter the group for they thrived off the offended looks and annoyance that rolled off the other punters

26

like waves; it fuelled them. One by one they raised the shot glasses to their lips, knocking the amber liquid back in one fluid motion, the sting barely lasting before the flush of warmth spread from their stomachs and throughout their bodies. Spurred on by the alcohol claiming that they were greater than anyone else who'd lived, their rowdiness grew in intensity minute by minute, and right in the middle of it all stood Justin. He was being initiated, and slowly but surely he was passing every test they had in store for him, proving that he was more than the child they had first mistaken him for. He had potential, though not even he realised how easily they would manipulate that if given the opportunity.

Chapter Four

And there they sat again, the corner they had inhabited in earlier weeks now fully marked as theirs and theirs alone; a gang of rabid dogs pissing all over everything they felt belonged to them. Due to their numerous visits now, with Justin in tow, everyone knew exactly who they were and that they weren't to be messed with unless you were looking for a fight in short order. Huddled around like cackling witches, the lads were having a usual laugh and a joke, accompanied by a heated debate between Lloyd and George. An outsider might think they were riled up about an important matter, such as the terrible political parasites that were infesting the nation like a sweeping disease, but instead they were chatting about women. More to the point, whose potential conquest was better looking; Justin grinned as he positioned him comfortably enough to listen with ease.

"She was far fucking fitter than yours, mate!" Lloyd roared, unable to downplay his annoyance at George's persistence.

"Bullshit, her face looked like the backend of a fucking horse." Quipped back, their banter like an equally matched tennis match, only there was no skill on display here, unless skill counted as drunken arguing.

"Your missus was actually a fucking fella!" *Shots fired,* Justin mused as he and the others sat back and enjoyed the show, imaginary popcorn circulating the group. In a sharp retort, George exclaimed that Lloyd was an arsehole, a spare obscenity or two added for good effect. Finally, as if he was determined to finish the pointless battle, Lloyd settled it with-

"Rather that than fucking an arsehole."

Silence rung like the twang of metal as the men glared at each other, mock seething mixed in with real irritation, and then, when it seemed like the soundless void would continue to grow, the rest of the guys erupted into a chorus of merriment then signalled the end of the debate. To Justin, still new to the banter of these men, he felt that Lloyd had managed to steal the victory, but nobody discussed it to find out, instead it was unspoken between them all. Although they were all caught up in the web of chortling, Milton stayed his laughter as he eyed the bar with intense curiosity and mischief lighting up his eyes. Leaning against the bar, her flashes of a devilish smile calling to them every now and then as she stared at them, stood an older woman quietly sipping her drink. Despite her seasoned appearance, the woman was quite beautiful in a stereotypical sort of way: the dyed blonde hair and painted features screamed femme fatale, although her years somewhat diminished the otherwise immaculate rendition.

Unbeknownst to Justin and Kevin, both of whom were embroiled into a casual catch up after another draining week, Milton had been whispering into Lloyd's nearest ear, a wicked sneer curling the corners of his mouth. The others followed suit, all leaning in and playing the game of Chinese whispers, with the teenager and his friend, outsiders yet to be looking in. Lloyd, having assumed some sort of command over the hisses of hushed tones, turned his attention to Justin. "Justin… Justin…" Grabbed from the conversation he had been engaged with, he paused and looked inquiringly at the man, a questioning painted on his face.

"Yeah?"

"Have you seen her?" He points to the woman at the bar, his accusing finger unseen by her roaming eyes; using the bony digit as a guide, Justin too averts his attention over to the woman. The difference being that this time, as if she *knew*, the lady turned those seductive eyes onto the young boy and unleashed her persuasive smile. He was certain it had lured many before, such

29

was its power, and yet he failed to see where his companion could be going with this… "Her?"

"Yeah. So, what do you think?"

"She's alright."

It appeared that it wasn't just young Justin who was confused by the interrogation, for Kevin arched his eyebrows as he gazed at Milton suspiciously, the question he wanted to ask ready to spew from his sealed lips. Even though he could normally follow the guys with ease, sometimes knowing what they planned before they did properly, on this occasion he was stumped. And that irked him a little. He didn't like being left out, even on a casual subject like this one; he wanted in on everything, it was *his right*. "Why do you-?"

"Shut up, you twat!" Hissed Milton, desperate to keep mum, especially in the face of Justin. Surprisingly, Justin still remained clueless about it all, while Kevin, although having to piece it together unaided, soon figured out exactly what was planned. It was one of their tests, a stupid test, but one that they would all enjoy… except Justin. Obliviously, Justin asked "What about her?"

"What about her," Frankie cut in, a convincing look of disgusted shock claiming his expression. "what about her? Don't you want to have a fucking woman like that?" Before he answered, Justin spotted Milton and Lloyd conferring, their chuckles alerting him that something fishy was going on here. He summarised that, while they could be genuine in thinking he liked this woman, he doubted they would be pissing their pants about it unless they were setting him up. Still, he decided to play his part well, his innocence fooling them all.

"I wouldn't mind her." Hardly a lie if he was totally honest.

His response spurred Lloyd on, his hungry eyes excited by how well Justin was playing into his game, he had expected it to be harder than this… "You should fucking chat her up."

"Yeah," shot in Milton. "see if you can get your end away with her." They all nodded in encouragement, which Justin found laughable – how did they think they weren't obvious? There were plenty of women in the pub, and although she was the closest, she wasn't necessarily the most obvious target.

"Yeah right." was all he could manage to mumble, now finding it difficult to seem so unsure and confused when he had sussed them. In an attempt to rile the arrogance in him, for George was sure all young men had it, he had when he had been Justin's age, he jabbed lightly "You afraid to give it a shot?"

"No…"

"Then what's stopping you?"

"Yeah go on, mate, show us what you're made of." It was Kevin who cut in, which surprised Justin. Then again, he wondered whether it should, Justin was still new to them and had yet to fully prove himself as one of the lads. Yes he had come along and been brought in by Kevin, but he doubted that mattered much to the other guys; they might hang with Kevin and happily allow him to appoint himself as a leader, but they by no means worshipped him. He was really his own God, no one else's, though he wasn't sure that Kevin had figured that out yet, or maybe he had and preferred denial.

Regardless of how they actually saw Kevin within their ranks, whether he was the leader of the pack or simply a wannabe, the men used his confirmation as a lead into some loud chanting, their fists pounding the table in a primal drumroll. Deafening was an understatement, every bang sounded louder than the last, and mixed in with their throaty slurred cheers it proceeded to escalate. In a mock surrender of defeat, Justin raised his hands up meekly in an attempt to simmer down their unbearable peer pressure. "Alright, alright you wankers." Even though this was futile for he already knew what was happening, he had no choice but to continue down the path they had laid out so lovingly for

31

him. As he stood and turned his back to them, he allowed himself the briefest of smiles – they were going to look the idiots not him, and he couldn't wait for the unveiling.

As he shuffled forward in what looked to them as a lamb going to slaughter, their bated breaths and muffled giggles difficult to suppress, Justin crossed the space between himself and the woman.

"Do you think he realises?" Milton squeezed out, a small chuckle wriggling its way out and opening up the floodgates for all the others; their booming sniggers were hardly subtle, so Justin wagered they either thought him stupid or simply naive. Kevin managed to suppress his chortling enough to say "Well, he'll soon release when they fuck and she asks for payment." much to the joy of the others who upped the ante on their laughing to the point where it almost sounded false, similar to what you hear on old sit-coms. As they observed they couldn't help but eye Justin as he chatted to her, all of them tottering off their seats to get a good glimpse of the show. "Watch… watch…" they hissed.

The woman engrossed in the young man before her responded politely, listening intently to what Justin had to say, every now and then turning to the men across the bar and laughing. To the lads it looked as if she were laughing with them, in on their joke and playing along, with poor Justin oblivious, little do they know that she's laughing *at* them. Locked onto them like a sniper staking his unknowing prey, Kevin and his friends shivered with delight as they watched their young newcomer kiss the woman. Amused that all was going in their favour, the convulsions started once more and work their way through the group like a Mexican wave. Nonetheless, despite the noise ringing in the interlocked couples' ears, they continued their kiss, the passion intense and fierce. "Poor lad, he won't know what's hit him when he finds out," Kevin muttered, not at all concerned for his friend, but more entertained by how hilarious it'd be when Justin was left with egg on his face for being such a trusting fool.

Breaking from the embrace, they watched as the youth teased with one last lingering kiss, before strolling over and plonking himself down in his seat once more. The stifled howls gave him no end of joy as he sat there, poker faced, waiting for them to poke, prod and make fun, knowing all too well they'd look the fools. He would be a legend to them, having played them at their own game and beat them, they'd accept him openly now, no more kid this and baby talking, he'd be an equal. Lost in thought he almost missed what George was asking him, his throaty tones small in comparison to the ringing fits of giggles, "So then, how much did that chat cost you, Jus-TEEN?" the last four letters of his name drawn out, intended to highlight how childish he was in the presence of all these wise men. The smile that curled nervously at his lips was something he had to hold in check, the willpower readily waning.

"Only a few drinks."

"What?!" Although he didn't shout it, the force behind the probing was as sharp as an angry tongue, George evidently dumbfounded at this nonchalant reply.

On cue the barman entered, dutiful in his delivery of the punchline that all the men hadn't seen coming, a smile on his features that rivalled that of Justin's; he was delighted that the teen had tricked him. His hearty voice, rich and friendly but able to be stern at a moments notice, instructed them to drink up as he placed the tray down, all the glasses shimmering gems in the dim light. Even though there was confusion in their ranks, the glittering liquid called to them all, and so it was Kevin who finally broke and asked who purchased their round of drinks to a grinning Justin.

"She did." Came the smug reply as he turned slightly to look at the woman, a brief wink exchanged between the two of them.

"What?"

"I know her, from last weekend." And there it was, that beautiful moment he had been waiting for since they had spurred him on

33

to chat her up. Those usually insignificant words sounded sweeter than ever, and gave him such satisfaction he felt that sex with the prostitute wouldn't have been as good as this. Sex was sex, whereas this was a victory.

In turn, in a motion that mimicked chinese whispers, the men turned to look at one another, an expression of surprise molding their features. They didn't look annoyed, nor did they look blown away, no, it was a more gentle win for Justin, and one that appeared to have impressed them. Milton murmured a "fucking hell", while George exclaimed, although it really wasn't needed, that the son of a bitch had played them. It sunk in for mere seconds, and then the alcohol fuelled hooting reared its ugly head yet again, Justin was the conductor, and oh did it feel good.

***

Much to their dismay, the group had had to say goodnight to the comforts of the pub as the barman had politely, but firmly, informed them that it was closing time. They hadn't put up much of a fight, for they had been ready for a change of scenery, a rush from an alternative source. Now they were down a sleeping street of some estate, all of them walking in perfect unison, a reenactment of the *Reservoir Dogs*, though they were all pissed up and lost in their drunken jokes rather than having stylish purpose. Still, the idea that they came close to that made Justin feel unstoppable. Even in the face of flashing lights from nearby houses, accompanied by shouts for them to be quiet, didn't deter him from his contentment; after months, years, of trying to figure out what the hell his life was about, he finally felt like he had discovered his scene. Yes, it wasn't for everyone, his mind presented a disapproving Eddie frowning at him, but it was for *him*.

Reaching the last of the bottles to his lips, Justin took a swig of the bitter ale, caught up in the motions. Although he was switched off, Milton was very much on high alert as an oncoming group came into view further down the road. Even though he couldn't strain his eyes enough to determine their features, he whispered his warning to the others, quietly readying them for a battle. "Fucking hell... look out." Confused, Justin let the bottle leave his lips for his eyes to look beyond their group, to the descending 'threat'; they appeared to be several cocky youths full of swagger strutting towards them, their attitudes suffocating the night air. Immediately, for reasons he couldn't quite pinpoint, he disliked them. Although Kevin sensed the disdain colouring Justin, he couldn't help but instruct him to watch out – he didn't want to be dragging the boy to hospital, or having to tell his family how he had been responsible for their son being hurt. At least that's what he tried to tell himself, really he just didn't want to babysit when there was potential action on their horizon. While Kevin had been pretending to care, the leader of the pack, the one with the baggiest jeans and most arrogant face, had stepped forward while his mates fanned out like synchronized swimmers.

Justin, a boy who had heard about gangs facing off like this but had never been a witness, watched mesmerised as the lead guy roared in their faces, his confidence knowing no bounds and certainly not respect. "Move the fuck out of our way, dickheads!" He spat, spittle flying through the crackling air, the only thing moving despite the two tribes now glaring heatedly at one another. *What is his deal,* Justin asked himself, unable to fathom why the little shit couldn't walk around them, or even cross the road, *it's not like he can't walk by. Dick.* In spite of his increasing urge to want to punch and kick his way through the youths in front, he would have been happy to walk away, merely closing his ears to their false threats of violence. They were probably all talk anyway, or they definitely seemed to be. Sadly however, Milton had other plans for he had been seething since catching their sight in the distance, and wasn't at all ready to walk away from this. "Fuck you, you gobby cunt!"

As if that hadn't escalated the situation enough, the youngster screamed for them to all do one before swiping a blade through the air, his target Milton. Without so much as a second thought, and fearing for another's life, Justin aimed the bottle he had been holding at the teen, the glass hitting its mark effortlessly. Even though the bottle didn't smash upon impact, the *clunk* it made as it pounded into thin flesh covering thick skull was harsh enough to cause the boy to crumple to the floor. Like a house of cards caught in the breeze, it fell down into a messy pile, his gang watching with wide eyes, their reflexes dulled by the unexpected introduction of a bottle into the mix.

Seizing their chance to attack and get the jump on the others, Kevin and his cronies all charged forward into the fray, their fists landing into faces and other fleshy areas exposed to them. They had a fury that was all their own, and that initially frightened Justin as he watched on, a spectator at a bloody show in two minds of whether to continue being a bystander or throw himself in too. It wasn't that he didn't want to help out his friends, but more that he had no idea where to start, such was the chaos before him. To his left Kevin was cracking the delicate bones of a boy's face, the marrow rich skeleton unable to withstand such punishment, while across from that was Frankie and George huddled around a trembling body on the ground, their feet relentlessly flying in and out. It was rhythmic in how they swung their legs, the sack of skin and bones curling into a ball taking blow after blow, their shoe tips bringing blood bubbling to the surface, the tender flesh already succumbing to the beginnings of yellow bruising from the intense onslaught.

That wasn't the worst though, for it was Milton that was by far the most crazed of them all; a crazed beast screaming as he took on any who still stood in his way. It was a psychotic show that rivalled that of anything he'd ever seen before, and definitely caused Justin to question whether horror stories of evil ghosts could ever compare to the rage of mankind. In stark contrast, but still as unnerving as the furious men barking before him, was Lloyd, laughing with childish joy as he watched it all, his personal play of blood, screams, and echoing bone cracks. Normally, a bystander such as young Justin would see all this and think that it signaled the time to leave, but not him, no, he wanted to be in there. The decision was made, and while he had roamed his eyes over the scene before, it had only taken a matter of minutes for him to become a thug like them.

Regardless of the mix of flailing legs and arms, it didn't take him long to set his sights on one of the rival gang members, a boy that was set to lunge at Milton. Acting on raw instinct, a normally untapped part of his psyche, Justin rushed and kicked the middle of the turned back, his foot landing swiftly but firm, the victim toppling forward and smacking the ground with a slick slap, crimson trickling from a new wound. Readying himself for another round, Justin strode over and lifted his right foot, ready to stamp out the boy of a similar age sprawled underneath him, when flashes of red and blue flooded his vision. As if they received a jolt of electric, all of them stopped and turned their attention to the siren that was now accompanying the nearing colours, a high pitched melody that injected a new fear into their veins. "POLICE!" Lloyd screeched, bodies already moving in front and to the side of him as they all parted like rats seeking the comfort of darkness.

Chapter Five

The narrow opening provided them a quick getaway, the lights pulsating faster and brighter, the police ready to swarm the area and take in the brutality of the broken teenagers on the ground, all of them swollen eyed and puffy faced, their egotism caking the pavement alongside their blood and spit. It's a depressing and yet awesome scene that the officers couldn't help but scan cautiously, the worry etched into their very fibre that they needed to remain alert while they investigated, for the perpetrators could return at any moment.

Although Kevin's group ambled down dirty alleyways filled with vomit and urine, a stench of garbage attacking their nasal passages, all of them couldn't hold back the wave of relief that was waving over them. They had just had an epic albeit unexpected brawl, and they had won, and most importantly, they had escaped the wrath of the authorities. Justin could scarcely believe their fortune, and was the first to laugh as they rushed towards his estate, all of them having forgotten the trouble they had nearly landed themselves in. When the estate came into full view, the mobilised herd finally slowed, allowing them all a chance to catch their breaths.

Slightly quieter than before, Justin shuffled up to his front door and began to get the key in the lock, while the lads looked at him expectantly, waiting for him to comment on the night's events. They didn't wait long, for as soon as the reassuring *click* sounded from the door, their youngest member faced them with an exhilarated grin clutched to his sweaty face. "That was fucking amazing!" The beam of his expression, mixed with the heady words of an adrenaline filled teenager was music to the group's ears, all of them pleased that they had turned the boy into one of them. Not just a drinking buddy, but a hooligan like them, the only difference being that he didn't know he'd graduated to the latter just yet. Out of all of the men stood outside the sorry flat, it was Kevin who was most impressed with Justin. "I'm glad you had a good time," he smiled, a wicked glint in his eyes that was hidden by the blackness of the night and lost on the glazed over looks of his excited friends.

"Joining us again?" George asked.

"Fucking hope so." Milton cut across, his primary focus on the teen and him alone.

The idea of being out with them all again sounded great, and the prospects of another fight springing up when they left the pub next weekend was the cherry on top of a large cake. It felt like getting a deal, a two for one: go out with your mates (*they're my mates, right?*) and knock back a couple of drinks, then head off out and see which set of idiots wants to challenge them next. Sure, they may not come across anyone and end up having a quiet stroll home, but they could also bump into another group of riled up fools and pump up their fists yet again; the unknown was as good as the fight. "Yeah, definitely – the pub again?" Justin asked, not even considering they may hang out elsewhere for he hadn't been taken anywhere else over the course of their last few meet ups.

"Nah, fuck that," Milton scoffed while he racked his brains for another place to suggest; it didn't take him long to come up with the perfect solution. "You like footy?"

As anyone who knew Justin and his family situation would know, football and him didn't exactly mix well. It wasn't that he didn't like the sport, in fact he loved it, but it was that it reminded him so much of his drunk dad stumbling in and targeting his wife. Nonetheless, while he had always maintained a distance between himself and matches, he couldn't stop himself from declaring his love for the beautiful game. Ultimately, he wasn't his dad and wasn't necessarily destined to turn into a lout like him when at a match, so he didn't see an issue with him going to watch a game. An aspect that Lloyd agreed with wholeheartedly, despite not knowing anything about what plagued the boy's homelife. "We're seeing a game on Saturday, so why don't you come along?" And, as if the invitation alone wasn't enough, Frankie piped up and added "We could do with someone like you."

How could he say no to all of that? He was a wanted man, a needed member of the group, and without him they weren't their functioning unit. They didn't work, or at least that's what he whispered to himself as he nodded his head while his hands absentmindedly pushed open the front door.

"I'll give you a bell about it," Kevin promised. "So piss off home now." Justin gave a warm laugh as he started to walk inside, happy that he could have a laugh with them all; that sense of belonging engulfing him like a mother's embrace. Even if alarm bells had sounded, which they hadn't since his first meeting with them, he doubted he'd have listened, so strong was their influence on him. He hadn't known them long, but he already knew he'd do anything to make them like him more, and while they were all surrounding him he wouldn't let that omission bother him. "Oh yeah, we've been talking. If you join us, you need a different name." Before their leader had fully finished, all of the others nodded in unison, with Lloyd adding, without consideration for Justin's feelings – "A tougher name, as Justin makes you sound like a bender."

A gay, my name makes me sound like a homo?! He couldn't help but be mildly insulted, his mouth already spitting out a blunt "Fuck off" to their playground comments, and yet what they said bothered him. He wanted to be tough, like them, hell, he *was* so why couldn't they see it? In an attempt to try and soften the blow of this realisation that his Christian name apparently screamed big massive homosexuality, similar to a neon sign, Milton added sombrely that his mate had a point, and that the name just wasn't manly enough for their group. As if somewhere someone had written a list of significant importance stating, quite plainly, what names emasculated a boy and what didn't; never did you hear that a girls name was too butch or too feminine. Even though he knew that allowing such opinions made him sound like a privileged idiot, and that Danielle would have slapped him silly if he had dared to utter it, he thought how lucky women were.

"Jay. We'll call you Jay." Justin heard as Kevin revealed the new name, much like he'd finally decided what his favourite puppy should be called. Not that he'd say it, but the whole thing was humiliating, however instead of showing that sign of weakness, he shrugged his now tired shoulders as he moved further into the flat's hallway. In reality though, what could he do without incurring the wrath of his new gang? Sure he could kick up a stink and whine and bawl about how a name didn't mean anything but actions did, but like that point even held validity among the men he was trying to impress. They weren't academic beings who desired debate and longed for new insight, but were men who enjoyed the familiarity of their own truths. "Now bugger off!" Kevin cackled, necessarily, the laughter that followed cut short by the sound of the door resting back into its frame, the outside world now locked behind its protection for the night.

The warmth that had gripped Justin so profusely was lingering, and it was a pleasant sensation to experience as he walked through his cold home, all warmth they should have resided there nowhere to be found. How could a home offer that level of intimacy when all that lived there was despair and dysfunction? Trying to shake his dark thoughts away, he allows his tired body to carry him into the living room and over to the window. Looking out at the fading night, and the tinges of colour leaking onto the horizon and into the sky, Justin paused to give a glance to his sleeping mum on the settee, her black eye more intense than the changing hues

41

outside. And that was when the last ebs of happiness seeped out of him, and the events of the night, his acceptance of explosive progression into Kevin's fold, lay forgotten at the bottom of his raging mind, his dad now at the fore.

Deep down he knew he should let it go, allow the anger to wash over him and then disappear, like his mother did every time a fist pummeled her vulnerable self, but he can't. He couldn't stand there, looking at her and ignore the fact this his dad was sleeping peacefully above them both, no shame to be found for his actions that damage a family that will never be whole. Without even noticing, it wasn't until his eyes fell upon his father's form instead of his mum's that he realised he'd climbed the stairs and entered their bedroom. Silently he stood there, eyes ablaze and his body shaking – what he wouldn't give to wake up and that horrid man be gone from their lives. While he knew he could stomp and storm about the room, his dad too consumed by the booze to even register what was happening, Justin couldn't bring himself to waste that much energy on a waste of space like him. So alternatively he walked out of the dank cave of the slumbering monster, travelled into the recesses of his room, and willed sleep to take him how it had his parents.

Chapter Six

The sun that he had seen ready itself to flood through drawn shades and announce the morning to the world, hung high in the sky, although its rays weren't as brilliant as they should have been. Not that lack of illuminosity mattered for he was trapped inside the grubby corridors of the local shopping centre, where the sunlight never ventured and only artificial light was in abundance. Despite the dismissal environment they all found themselves in, shoppers and their trading counterparts went about business, ants in a commodity invested hive, their lives all grand on the outside and despairingly shit on the inside. He hated that he was a part of the milling bugs, but Eddie had wanted to have a catch up, and he had to admit that anywhere other than home was better, even if that plan had involved torture, such was his contempt for his house.

When he had peeled open his groggy eyes, stained with the dregs of alcohol, sleepiness, and more importantly, the lingering sheen of a post adrenaline high, he didn't want to admit to anyone, least of all himself, that there had been a stinging in his eyes from tears that still waited to freely fall. That had been the extent of his disgust when he had looked upon his slumbering dad in the early hours. Even though he had screamed for sleep to claim him, to drag him down into the darkness so deep that no dreams dared stir, sleep had been cruel and left him with his thoughts. And those thoughts had gone to his father.

All too often in the minutes that ticked away as blissful ignorance refused to save him, Justin considered walking back into the bedroom that had once belonged to both parents,

43

and cracking the skull of his dad like he'd wanted to those thugs on the street. The image had been so powerful and consuming; flashes of blood, torn skin and pained howls for help, and all of it had been delightful on the ears. He honestly didn't see himself as a violent young man, even despite the episode he'd experienced with Kevin and co a short time ago. However, he couldn't escape the idea that a vile creature lived within him that caused him to ignite with hatred. Even calling it hatred didn't do it justice, for that implied that he still held some emotion close to love towards his dad, and that certainly wasn't true after years as a spectator to his mum's regular beatings. No, the hostility he felt couldn't be pinned down and named, such was its enigma.

But while his bloodlust for the man who helped create him was formidable and burdensome, he was determined never to break the little resolve he had because he knew his mother wouldn't be able to cope. She was a prison of a stronger cell than him, and yet she continued to weather it and accept her life as gospel, as if God had decided long ago that she should never try to force her way out of the life he had crafted for her, shit or not. Well, that wasn't what he would do. He would never ever lay down his life to live so miserably, and not for a man that hadn't given him anything but blighted memories. That was why, when Eddie had called and suggested they meet, he had jumped at the chance like a girl surprised to be asked to the school dance. Although he would have preferred to have heard from Kevin, his disappointment hadn't remained with him long, after all, he was seeing his guys soon, and that was guaranteed to be a day to remember. Justin had smiled as he'd closed the front door, the sound of the mechanism *clicking* into place, a sound that hailed safety from his ominous home once more.

Now, in the hellhole of consumerism, the two joined the throngs of others spilling out of the guts of modernity to reveal secrets and be in on the latest gossip; Justin was filling his friend in on the episode from the night before. To outsiders observing the two, they would be able to recognise two palpable emotions at play between the two men: one of excitement and the other of concern. Nonetheless, despite his disinterest in fights and the lives of yobs, Eddie dutifully listened to his friend, waiting for his chance to impart some much needed advice. Or that had been his plan, but the moment his youthful companion mentioned having fought himself, that peaked Eddie's interest to the point where he couldn't remain silent anymore. "A fight?" Was all he could manage, but he felt it sufficed. Taken aback by his stupid question, Justin carried on -

"Yeah, a bunch of local fucking youths, right trouble making arseholes. We put them in their place." He finished smugly, a sneer worn upon his face that didn't suit him at all, for it wasn't a face he'd usually wear but one that belonged to the likes of Kevin. Troubled was an understatement when Eddie looked at his friend, and yet he couldn't let go of the irritation that was boiling below the surface of his usually calm exterior.

"Really?"

"Really what?" Enquired Justin, put out that Eddie wasn't as in awe as he should be.

"I said 'really', as in did you really put them in their place, or do you think one of them is having the exact same conversation as you today?"

In spite of the fact that Justin knew that his mate had more than a relevant point, he didn't want to give him the satisfaction of knowing, for he was irked at how ready Eddie was to steal the fun away from the previous evening. Although violence wasn't an action he felt was perfectly acceptable, he also had the conflicting viewpoint that on occasion it was necessary. His dad was the unspoken example that he would never divulge.

It wasn't the first time that the boy (and that's how he saw himself when Eddie lorded age over him) felt conflicted and lost between a rock and a hard place, cliche as it was for him to think. In one corner he had 'Jay', his new persona that was badass, cool, and in with the crowd, and in the other he had boring old Justin, a teenager missing out on the excitement of the world because of fear instilled by another. Not that it really was just Eddie's fear pushed onto him, for he too had a tiny bubble welling up with concern that he was choosing to overlook and pretend didn't exist. He didn't want to be that nobody scum that had amounted to nothing, that had never made a name for himself, and yet he didn't want to be the guy that everyone recoiled from because he was a force to be scared of. Then again, and much to his Justin sided thought processes, he didn't want to be like Ed, a man that had neatly slotted into middle age life of stereotypical bliss.

Justin couldn't help but wonder whether Eddie would have preferred Kevin, Milton, Frankie, George, and Lloyd to be hurt rather than having stood their ground. "What the fuck are you talking about?" Justin spat, resembling Kevin way more than Eddie felt comfortable with. How he saw it, there was a transition underway, even if Justin wasn't aware of it himself, and whether he had to fight Justin tooth and nail, he didn't want his friend to end up like Kevin.

Certain that replying with a question of how stupid Justin was would cause more problems, Eddie decided to pause for a moment and look into a nearby shop window, the affluent jewellery twinkling and tempting all that walked by, the majority of which unable to afford such a hefty price tag. They were exquisite pieces, and he was sure his latest payday would cover a couple of the jewels he saw, but while he genuinely started to examine the pieces through the pane of glass, he could feel the heat rolling off the teen behind him, and felt it was best to not leave him seething for much longer. Eddie tried to tell himself it was because he didn't want to upset a dear chum, but in truth he was scared that Justin would get into such a state that he'd act out in a public place. A night time brawl was bad enough, but one in broad daylight would attract way too much attention, and he doubted he would be able to excuse Justin's actions; violence in London, while expected by many, wasn't overly tolerated by the police. In actuality, he was sure the authorities were even harsher than most about fighting because of how much stick they normally got from news readers and the public. "What I'm talking about, Justin, is you fucking about and wasting your time with people like Kevin."

In spite of attempting to avoid riling Justin further, the very mention of Kevin and waste in the same sentence proved a miscalculation on his part; now he had a hormonal, emotional teenager glaring at him with menace that belonged in folklores and not real life. The clench and unclench of his fist served as little of a distraction to how badly he wanted to throw himself at the 30 something man he usually called a close friend. Had he known that Eddie was this pathetic the whole time, or was the shine finally cracking and falling from the other he'd always looked up to. No, Ed would never be a name that everyone on the estate knew, despite how much they all delved into each other's business, but people that *did* know of him was aware how hard he'd worked to turn his life around and escape a path of drugs, violence, and prison. *Commendable*, Justin had thought in his slightly younger years, *how amazing to come back from being someone like dad.* But now? Now he thought his idol to be arrogant, far worse than what he accused Kevin of being. "You're just jealous." was the extent of what he could manage without completely offloading, and that he wanted to avoid.

Being taken aback wasn't what Ed had anticipated – he'd thought Justin would make a dig about him being old, not cool, something juvenile and without real meaning, but for him to make out as if Eddie was jealous was astounding. He didn't in any shape or form, and would never in his whole life, harbour any jealousy towards the leader of their pack. Why would he? He'd been pretty big in his *own group*, and look where that had got him. "No… I'm really not, I can promise you that."

"Then what's the problem?" was spat back with all the fury of youthful speed and need to understand.

"Justin…"

"Jay."

Oh for fuck's sake! Eddie was borderline shaking with anger himself now, for it was like talking to a stranger, and it was one he didn't particularly like. Not only was he having to listen to such drivel about the fun of hurting others, coupled with how wonderful a group of men are who should know better, he now had to contend with a name change that he was certain Justin wouldn't have asked for. *Jay*, it sounded as smarmy as Kev and his monkeys. About all he could manage to reply with was an exasperated "what?", before eyeing Justin as a lost cause. He vaguely heard the boy state that Jay was his new name, as if suddenly it was okay to be treated like a dog, and could do little but allow the words to echo around his head. Each syllable stung. Even though he was all fired up and ready to retort back, he could do nothing more than shake his head and start to walk away, leaving his mate flailing about for a small time, and then running to catch up. Oh how Eddie wanted Justin to be keeping in step because he realised how foolish he was being, but age had taught him differently, and he knew that Justin – Jay – was annoyed at not getting a response.

"What's the fucking problem?" At last broke the uneasy silence that had come between them, though right now both secretly prepared the silence. Eddie rounded with speed that Justin staggered back slightly, a rage in his eyes that was struggling to remain encased in its glossy confinement. "Who chose the name?" And now it was Justin that had to pause and contain himself; it was like they kept swapping roles in an unspoken fight for superiority.

"What?"

"I asked you who chose the name." Flat, unfeeling vocales slithered in his ear canals, and for the first time since they'd begun their disagreement, Justin felt genuine sadness that it was coming to this. It didn't diminish his resentment at present, but he doubted anyone could tame that beast right now for it was fuelled by multiple sources, with his so called friend just adding to a long list.

"I did."

"You're a real piss poor liar, *Justin.*"

That emphasis, that drawn out definition reminded him so much of the night before, when the guys had called him Jus-teen – to hear the same name pronounced so differently really hit home just how little a name meant when you looked at it logically. Nevertheless, while only a name, it was a symbol of change that he wanted more than anything. Eddie had watched a lot of Justin's life unfold, a miserable audience member in a depressing rendition of how awful council estates and their grimy lives can be. So how could he not comprehend why Justin wanted to ditch the persona of being another unfortunate soul, and to to become a name of meaning, of power? "Fuck's sake…" he breathed, drained of the ill temper that has sustained him for so long. "The estate isn't easy…"

"Don't give me that," and hearing that was like a slap across the face, a ninja attack you never saw coming. "I'm from the same fucking area. You don't see me making excuses, I made something of myself."

"What, being a rich twat?! Yeah, you really made something of yourself, didn't you?"

There was a lot of things that Eddie didn't mind being called, many of which went back to school days of teacher's making it clear in no uncertain terms that he would never amount to anything. And he could deal with them as they were a byproduct of life, a horrible part of the human condition, but one that was unavoidable nonetheless. However, while the majority of terms would never pierce his flesh, being called a rich twat was an exception, and why? Because it held resentment for having done well for himself, for having broken the consuming chains of a class system that buried so many. He hadn't been born into wealth, he'd had to work for it, and he had done so after nearly ruining what little life he had back then. Secondly, he wasn't *rich* by any stretch of the imagination; he was doing well for himself because he was working all hours he could and saving the rewards responsibly. Being financially secure and rich wasn't the same thing, yet rich was bandied about simply because such hatred of the upper classes still reigned in the ranks of poverty and despair.

"You need to listen to me, you need to listen and understand something." The monetary flat tone of his voice grabbed Justin long enough to be curious about the wisdom that Eddie thought he was about to share. "You need to steer clear of them, they're trouble and they'll only lead you to more trouble. I'm not asking you to do what *I* want, but I *am* asking you to NOT do what *they* want." All the while he had been watching Justin, he had been unable to gauge exactly what the other was feeling, for he seemed determined to keep every card of his deck close to his chest.

As for Justin, he understood what Eddie was saying, and if he was totally honest with himself, he didn't want to be seen as a mindless slave to anyone's whims other than his own. That being said, it was now his turn to deliver some truths.

"Maybe you should understand something as well; we're from the same estate, but for you it's different. You don't have a mum and dad like mine, instead you had it all. And yeah, the estate is shit, but when you got home you managed to escape it all. Me? It's hell out there and it's hell in here." Unsure of where to go from there, Justin shook his head with equal amounts of sorrow and annoyance, and started to walk away from Eddie, a sense that this was to be their last meeting in a while pulling at his emotions. Before he'd gotten too far away, he turned and gave into his teen angst, his parting words being that Eddie needed to grow up and grow some balls. Hardly a fitting finale, and definitely not one that was suited to the older male considering that he was of an age where he had grown up. Still, it was the only ammunition Justin had had to hand, and he had used it with gusto.

There were plenty of ways Eddie could have tried to resolve the tear in their companionship: he could have gone after him, called out a weak apology, hell, admitted he was wrong even though he wasn't, but he did none of those things. Instead he watched with a heavy heart as Justin walked away, being swallowed up by the crowds in quick succession. The sadness that followed him as he resumed his rounds of the mall was suffocating, despite his efforts to breathe against it. Although he didn't want to stare it in the face, he couldn't break free of the knowledge that he had lost the boy he'd once known, a child that had maintained brightness even though his dad had inflicted horrors. That lost cause he had been watching had finally gone into the abyss, and he couldn't follow him to that dark place, as much as he wanted to.

Chapter Seven

The news didn't do it justice. The hype, the pounding of valiant hearts and anticipation, they were all elements that television couldn't translate to the viewer.

Looming large on the landscape, the football stadium was as awe inspiring as it was foreboding, for it held so much promise and yet the potential for so much anger as well; it was a conduit that could be used for good or ill depending on how events panned out. Even when it was two second division teams such as the ones driven on the coaches today, the atmosphere was as physical as any person you stood next to in the queues to get inside. As for the inside of the heaving monster, that was something else. You couldn't move a muscle for every type of fan was sat or standing, their eyes fixated on the pitch below and the action that was dancing from one side to the next.

And then there was the chanting. Insistent and unrelenting, there was a hum of battle that you couldn't close your ears to, and that invaded every fibre of your being. It felt like you were staring a wild animal in the face and choosing to surrender to your inevitable death, such was its demanding intensity. That being said, the way the noise carried itself from person to person, convincing you to add your voice to the loud volumes despite better judgement, that was an element you couldn't not enjoy.

The Manchester fans that were at the opposite end spent the better part of their time spewing all sorts of abuse towards the London stands, which was where Justin and Kevin had been sat, the rest of the lads nearby, being as entertained as everyone else beside and beyond them. It didn't matter that the cheers mixed in with the boos, and that they got lost in the sea of other chants and screams, for it all sounded like a loud racket in the end. While each of the others were watching and shouting like any good fan, Justin instead was engrossed in explaining what had happened with Eddie in the shopping complex.

Each yell was more strangled than the next, their vocal chords struggling to keep up with the continued pitch of tones. "Well, fuck him then, he sounds like a fucking prick!" *Always and forever to the point*, Justin mused, and yet he felt the sudden and uncontrollable urge to defend Eddie, even though they hadn't spoken since their spat. "He isn't that bad!" Funnily enough, he wasn't convincing himself when he said it, so why he thought he would convince Kevin was beyond him, but still the words had left his mouth all the same.

What made the conversation all the more surreal was that Kevin turned to look at Justin with the same amount of force and determination as Eddie had, the action mirrored him so well that he couldn't help but compare the two. Yes, they were totally different, but they behaved the same when it came to Justin – they wanted to pull him in different directions, even if they made out otherwise. Their eyes locked, Kevin imparted his words of venom, not wisdom, though they spoke to Justin on a level that Ed never could or had. "Really? You're having a laugh aren't you? Fucking arshole trying to tell you what to do?!" He waved his hands around as if the very thought disgusted him. "What gives him the right to do that?!" Kevin finished, his eyes bulging from their sockets in a manner that would undoubtedly alarm any doctors sat in the crowds.

"I suppose." Justin replied; *he does have a point – Eddie doesn't have the right to tell me what to do, he's my friend, not my parent.*

"I fucking *know*! One thing you will know about me, Justin: I will never ever try to tell you what to do. A man must live his own path. Always." Maybe it was the atmosphere, the raw intensity of passion coming from all sides, but in that moment, in that brief space of time, Justin believed Kevin and his sincerity.

Being caught up in the moment didn't last long though, for the crowd jumped to its feet and a roar so primal ripped through every single stadium member. At first Justin wasn't certain where the commotion had come from, but then when he had allowed his gaze to fall upon the pitch it had all made sense. The London team had formed into a strong attack formation, rushing towards the ball and the opposition; it wasn't graceful, it was hard and fast, the only aim to steal the ball from the clutches of the other team. By any means necessary, although that latter omission was a silent decision among both teams.

The closer they got to the ball, to beating the Manchester side, the louder the noise became, the bass everyone's heartbeat going into overtime as their team got ever closer to that prime position. Sensing that defeat could be swift, the opposition tried their best to defend themselves, all of them desperate to send their best men forward to protect the ball. It was a rather pitiful display, that much they could all agree on; they scrambled more than they ran, the fear of loss driving them on yet causing them to make mistakes. And yet, somehow, one of the strikers had managed to land a sliding tackle that slammed into an unsuspecting London player, the footballer taken clean off of his feet and square onto the ground, the *crunch* heard as far as the upper stands.

The outrage that swelled with the crowd now was something that Justin couldn't stop himself from becoming a part of – he was no longer able to sit and watch, he was now fully invested, one of the team's backers. And his team had just suffered an injustice that the referee seemed indifferent about, as if it never happened, which in turn caused everyone around Justin in the London stands to heckle with greater determination. That lack of penalty, the removal of justice when it was due, was the final straw for the rabid fans slobbering at the mouth with the spittle of a temper that was ready to spill onto the pitch. Whatever dignity had been remaining, and Justin wasn't sure that there had been any to begin with, soon disappeared when the match played on, many of the Manchester lads looking thoroughly satisfied with themselves.

Every man was frustrated, their playful jibes now turned into full scale attacks that left no holds barred – from race, to family, to wealth, everything was thrown at the opposition. However, out of all the people stood booming out to the sky, it was Kevin that Justin noticed had the most irritated scowl and sneer of all. His face was one that belonged in a tale of revenge, not in the grounds of some football stadium. With the anger having been nurtured for the last several minutes, Kevin focused on a footballer to the side of the field, his legs stretched out to relieve muscle tension and ready him to go on and aid his team. Out of the corner of his eye, Justin watched as Kevin pulled his arm back and swung it forwards, the can it had once been holding now flying through the air toward its target down on the line. *Crack*. The projectile hit perfectly, crumpling against the head of the player, a signal for the mob that now inhabited the London side to move up and over the stands.

At first it was a one sided assault, a half hearted pitch invasion that the Manchester ranks wanted no part of, but steadily, as the mass grew in volume and finally reached the pitch, the non-violent bystanders were unable to remain idle. Matching the ferocity of the Londoners, every Manchester spectator and player entered into the fray, teeth bared and arms held high as weapons when no other objects were to hand. The swarm of fans, helped along by the brutal concoction of booze and rage flew across the field, anyone now a target to destroy. Men, women, even teens were all branded together and seen as one in the same: a person to take down.

When both tribes collided in the middle, the individuals that had relied on their own brute strength up until now immediately felt outmatched by the beer cans, bottles, and concealed weapons that had now been brought into the game. A glint of shattered glass, a pointed end of a switchblade, all of them danced to the same beat of hatred that was without rationality or reason. Having been dragged into the rolling waves, Justin was left watching the scene unfold in slow motion, his mind struggling to decide on how best to proceed. He could stand and watch, he could also stand there and be beaten just as everyone else around him was suffering, or he could move and get involved. By joining the crowd, any bruise, broken bone or bloody nose he received was because he had been part of something, on his terms, not because he had stood like a coward and allowed himself to be destroyed alongside everyone else.

Breaking into a fit of laughter, he moved forward with cat like reflexes, the memories of the previous fight, Eddie, his dad, and his new friends all creating a giant ball of energy that only had one outlet: to fight. Now that the last of his caution had been thrown to the wind, discarded with inhibitions, Justin lost himself to the carnal need to hurt. Bizarrely though, even despite his lust for pain, he was unable to stop himself from looking over at Kevin, not sure whether it was reassurance he sought. Either way he got it, for Kevin matched the ugly beaming grin of Justin's with his own, the two of them lovers of destruction with a mutual understanding.

That smile was all he had needed, even when his environment had changed from the muddy grass of the stadium to the dank, grey cell of the local police station.

***

It had been so beautiful while it had lasted, a majestic mess that had fluidity to it despite its obvious chaos, and yet it had been sadly brought to end by the might of the police force. Not before it had taken a couple of their men down with it, a fact that delighted

Justin no end as he sat uncomfortably on the hard seat in the cell, his body now numb to the cold of the metal that held his weight.

The others had been lucky, they had managed to scram before the authorities had clamped down the hands on them, but not Justin, no, he had been too caught up in ripping the shit out of anything that moved that he had failed to see the oncoming blur of black and blue. Not that he minded in all honesty, for he felt that by having been caught, the guys had seen his true colours, the full extent of what he was capable of. He wasn't just some newbie who was looking to be them, he *was* them, and now they couldn't say shit to deny that fact. Or at least that's what he reasoned with himself as the lack of company proved a little too much for him to bare.

As if due to divine intervention (Justin knew that wasn't the reason why), the bleak door of his concrete box opened and a self righteous officer with a nose so far in the air it looked like he'd smelt a terrible odour, stepped inside. There was a look of utter contempt on his podgy face, the folds of hanging skin unable to hide the disgust that he wore so proudly. Really though, Justin wasn't surprised to see the man look at him so – he had just been involved in a massive football fight, not to mention the fact that he was from a particularly notorious estate in one of the shadiest parts of London. All in all it did little to instill a sense of worth. Not that he cared what the fat prick before him thought, for he was about to get released, and the man hiding behind his badge couldn't do a thing about it. "What?" He asked, a smirk threatening to spread across his face.

"Come on, you little shit, it's time to go."

"Okay." Is all he could muster without cackling, one of his hands reaching for his jacket as he strode past the officer and out into the freedom of London.

After a few corridors, and more snooty faces looking at him like shit on their shoes, Justin managed to locate the front doors to the station, the outside world a sight that made him want to weep, even though it looked gloomy and overcast. While its colours matched the cell he had been kept it, the fact that it allowed for more promise made it that much more appealing, the reality that it was still a prison for him conveniently forgotten as he sucked in a lungful of air. Before he was able to take another step, a shout from a surrounding car pulled at him and provoked him to look over.

The guys were all stood, smiling like cats who had gotten the cream lining their faces, all of them beaming with pride at Justin; easily offering the most praise was Kevin. If he hadn't have felt good already, seeing their approving faces, all of them looking at him like a legend, made it all worth it. As if to confirm what Justin was thinking, Kevin cheered that they should all go for drinks to celebrate, and who was he to say no when he so desperately wanted a drink after his spat doing jail time.

Chapter Eight

It felt like they'd only just been here, and in reality, that was quite close to the truth; a day at best separated their last excursion to the pub, making it a second home to Justin. While the others worked in regular jobs, where they played nice roles and smiled when they were meant to – like Kevin and his postman role, and all the lovely old dears thinking him a golden boy – Justin didn't have that other world. He had home, which he wanted to escape every waking minute. It wasn't the same for them, and in some ways it bothered him. That was for another time though, as the thumping music that was shaking the windows with timid vibrations kept stirring Justin from his thoughts and bringing him into the moment. And that present was all about boozing it with friends, accompanied by a ridiculous amount of savory snacks whilst wowing over how badass they'd all been during the showdown with the Manchester fans.

Huddled around the table, the group was enjoying a fine array of merriment while Justin attempted to fathom out how he'd managed to avoid a criminal record – what should have been a charge had only been a slap on the wrist and some stern expressions of disapproval. If that was how the police were doing it nowadays, Justin doubted they'd be putting an end to growing crime rates any time soon. Even though all this had been mentioned a hundred times over, he wasn't able to catch himself before letting the same question slip through his lips: "I just don't understand why I wasn't fucking charged."

Annoying as it was, the others could sort of understand why the boy was so surprised, for they too had been that naive and unknowing about criminal dealings before. Nonetheless, it didn't stop Kevin from feeling an unstoppable wave of annoyance that he found near impossible to keep hidden away. All he could manage, without losing his cool, was to ask what the point of it would be.

"Yeah," cut in George, his gruff accent sounding rougher than ever, like his Englishness was weighing more heavily on him today. "I mean, football rioters? They know they can't do anything about it, it's not like it's organised crime."

"Definitely nothing organised about us!" Milton lightheartedly joked before slurping at his pint, the others following like the pack of hyenas they'd become known for being. Hell, if they were silent that was when the owner of the pub started to panic.

They were never quiet though, not even when the air between them turned sour, just like it had done when Lloyd had piped up about the opposition's fans and the crews that had been dotted throughout the stadium's numbers. "Fucking Manc cunts – I didn't know they were tooling up down this fucking way." They all nodded in agreement, equally unhappy about the turn of events, whereas Justin simply sat there obvious in his confusion. "A crew?" He tepidly asked.

"The fucking worst." Lloyd replied. "They're Northern, they're hard, and they're fucking crazy." Not exactly what an up and coming member of the group wanted to hear when he was still so inexperienced in their world, even despite the two fights he'd been thoroughly involved with so far. Milton interjected before it sounded completely hopeless, "But we still made mincemeat out of them."

"Yeah… yeah we fucking did." Sounded Kevin with smug triumph.

"It's no good though."

This intrigued Justin upon hearing this, the rest of them had felt confident about how they had fared against their rivals, whereas Frankie seemed to be far removed from that level of complacency. Was it because he knew something they all didn't, had experience that would prove invaluable to them all, or did he merely like being the blackest cloud in the room? All these questions and many more were being entertained by Justin in a matter of seconds, his stare flitting from Kevin to George to Milton and then back to Frankie. Regardless of the lack of speech currently doing the rounds at the table, the juvenile member got the sense that the Frenchman's opinion wasn't a popular one, especially since he'd just challenged Kevin to a pissing contest of sorts. Whether they were all their own men or not, the postman by day thug by night leader of the group was clearly just that: the man in charge.

The fact that the hush was beginning to become louder than their giggles led Justin to break the silence and ask what he assumed everyone else thought – "Why's that?" An enquiry that George didn't like one bit, though not because of Justin, but because of Frankie creating an opening for the junior to have need to even ask.

"Jesus, Frankie, you're running your goddamn mouth off again." *Ah*, was all Justin could think as it felt like he was finally getting to grips with the full ins and outs of the gang, and their issues that had otherwise been concealed in earlier pub outings.

"No I am not, no, not at all." Now it was Milton's turn to add his thoughts to the budding argument flowering in their corner of drunken paradise, and he was less than diplomatic about it. "What are you trying to say you stupid French bastard?" Frankie looked from George to Milton, a eye roll exchanged mid turn before he continued on to explain his opinion on the Manchester crews. "They come here, and we outnumber them, and so we take them out easily. But then that crew gets to go home, and they still think they fought bravely or something like that."

"Fought bravely, what fucking planet do you live on?!" Followed by "Planet? I don't even think he lives in the same fucking galaxy."

All the while they laid out, and into Frankie, about how he was wrong, Kevin remained like a statue, only his breathing giving away that he was still one of the living. Justin had presumed that it was because he was displeased, in spite of the compelling argument Frankie was putting forward, but then he couldn't understand why the man hadn't said so? It wasn't like Kevin to remain mute for so long, or at least that had always been the way of things since Justin had known him, which wasn't that long when he thought about it.

What he wanted to do, but he most certainly wouldn't, was to ask Kevin whether he agreed with Frankie or not, for it was his thoughts that mattered most to the boy seeing as it had been him that had 'recruited' him. If he couldn't give him respect then what was the point in even following them and getting deeper into this world of… *what? What was this world anyways?* His brow crinkled as he looked at each of the men individually, taking in their age, appearance, and all the other menial things he had overlooked previously. *Eddie would know.*

"He has a point though doesn't he? He has a point."

That snapped Justin and everyone else from their verbal attack on Frankie, while he himself went from ridiculed freak to all knowing oracle in a simple 11 word sentence. Ironically, it was now George who allowed his mouth to run away with him having specifically poked fun at Frankie for that very reason. It seemed that it was okay to question Kevin if you were the one doing it, but if you were another of the group, well then you were open to being condemned as a cocky prick. "He does?!" His voice was strained with so much surprise that he sounded like he'd swallowed helium. In a day and evening that had been full of surprises, another landed in their laps when Kevin calmly explained why Frankie wasn't an arsehole but in fact they all were, while conveniently absolving himself.

"Think about it," He began, his voice thoughtful. "those fucking Manc crews can just come down this way all the time, get involved in barneys and lose." Justin couldn't help but note the smirk Kevin wore when he uttered the word 'lose'. "They don't care that they lose, they get a ruck and because they're outnumbered ten to one, nobody loses any street cred." His smirk now morphed into his trademark grin as he looked at his faithful flock with childish glee. "Imagine if we flipped it though."

Up until this point, Justin had felt that he was the only one that hadn't quite followed what Kevin was trying to say, with his only real takeaway thoughts being that his black mentor was mentally deranged. Thankfully though, and judging by how muddled George now was, it seemed that he wasn't alone. "Flipped it?" He heard the other guy ask.

"Yeah, if we went up there."

"Well… we'd fucking lose it as well, mate." Came the reasoned and instant response, no consideration or debate needed.

"No we won't…"

"Their fucking crews are fucking hard enough as it is, let alone when there's fucking hundreds of them!" Lloyd pointedly added, trying his hardest to highlight how lethal this encounter would be if they were all mad enough to go through with it. This was when Kevin finally looked like his veneer was taking blows it couldn't afford to, struggling to maintain the facade that he was completely a-ok with their backchat.

"Yeah… but I'm a fucking nutcase…" Nobody could deny that, that was for sure. "And you all share one thing in common with me: you truly don't give a fuck. They want to break bones. Us? We want to fucking destroy them."

Now there was genuine silence emitting from their table, and the barman nervously ventured a sneaky look in their direction to make sure someone wasn't being quietly beaten to death, or that a chair wasn't in mid flight towards his other punters. A relieved breath exhaled from his tight lungs as he thankfully witnessed that none of the scenarios he had just watched inside his head were happening. Meanwhile, at the actual table that had been under scrutiny, Lloyd mumbled a nervous "Fucking hell."

"Yeah. It would be fucking hell – for them. We go up there, take them out, get involved with the ruckus with their gangs. We'll fucking destroy them." Like a President finishing the greatest speech of his generation, Kevin raised his bottle and took a swig while he waited for everyone to catch up with him. It didn't take long, and Justin was right there with them, ready to throw it all in and charge up to Manchester and knock some heads together.

"I'll drink to that shit." Frankie cheered, all of them clinking and drinking, toasting a plan that had the markings of great potential.

Chapter Nine

Back in his shitty home, the one where his dad lurked and his mother wept, Justin was locked in his room blasting out the music that charged his soul and sung in his veins. Music was the key to life for him, as it was for many others; it gave meaning on low days, and provided extra joy on happier ones. It never judged him, never forgot him, and would never betray him and leave him alone to fend in this crap existence called life. Not even a lover could compare to what music could do for him, though he couldn't deny that a shag wouldn't be welcomed.

Although the tunes washed over him and through him, he wasn't idle in his enjoyment, and was instead lifting weights to bulk up and put some meat on his frame. Even though he liked to pretend (even to himself) that this was a routine he'd always carried out, he hadn't actually ever used these fitness accessories since buying them. They had been neglected, longing to be touched but always receiving the lightest of caresses before being placed back into the dusty home they stayed in. In addition to lying about how often he worked out, he also preferred to be economical with the truth when it came to the reason why he was abruptly exercising; it wasn't to do with the gang. Not one bit.

Despite his internal denial, getting used to the weights hadn't taken long at all, and for now he was stood near his window, pumping his arms in time to the music. It was only when he caught a brief glimpse of someone watching him from the street below his parent's flat that he stopped lifting. Luckily for him, or perhaps not considering the man had just seen his pained exercise face, it was Kevin who had been watching him. A wave of his hand signalled that Justin was needed out on the estate and not inside his bedroom, and so he dropped what he was doing, reached for his hoodie, and rushed to make his way outside, the music forgotten and playing for the empty home to savour. Not that leaving his playlist on mattered, it wasn't like his dad or mum could say anything about it – he had to listened to them shouting and bawling every other night, so the least they could do was put up with some gritty, angsty, 'fuck you, world' songs.

Having climbed down the flight of stairs, Justin was now through the front door, making his way towards his friend that, until now, he hadn't noticed was smoking. The smell coming from the cigarette was to die for, and Justin knew immediately that it wasn't no ordinary tobacco. That unmistakable scent made his mouth water, and he longed for the heady aroma and the release it carried to do more than invade his nasal passages. Noting the lad's longing gaze aimed at the joint, Kevin extended his hand and offered it up. "I thought you might like to join me." Came the forced casual statement.

"Fucking hell, definitely, mate." Justin rushed, gushing with gratefulness as he took the smoke from Kev and proceeded to lift it to his lips, his body already waiting for the sweet hit to come. As he took it in, relishing every moment of it, he looked at Kevin with further curiosity, positive that it wasn't simply a smoke that he'd wanted to share. "Fuck, that's good."

Kevin gave little other than a smile as a means of response, secretly enjoying the subtle power he managed to exert over Justin without the kid even realising; to him sharing a spliff seemed like acceptance, and in some respects it was, but it also was a means of getting the teen to do something he might usually be against. A joint between 'friends' was a prelude to asking for something more in return for having such faith in Justin, just the younger of the two wasn't aware of all the facts yet. He'd learn, just as every other member of any gang eventually learned. "I have a bloke

I buy from, it's fucking brilliant stuff." Justin grinned as the fix started to spread throughout his body, a relaxing sensation slowly easing the tension from his workout. "Fuck, it really is. So, is this all you wanted to show me?" *Ah, he's learning,* thought Kevin as he began to walk away, a sign for the newly christened Jay to follow. Obediently, Justin fell in line.

The walk was brief, and had led him to the local park, the equipment there rusted and old, neglected by a council crying out for financial help but never getting the fullest of what they required. What had once been a place where children could go and allow their family a brief respite from their mania, was now a ghost of its former self, closed and restricted from the public. It wasn't that nobody was allowed there as such, for the fencing around it hardly worked sufficiently as a keep out precaution, but it was a known estate rule that children should stay away. Only the most daring, or stupid, of the kids tended to break the rules to show off their worth to their peers.

Sat among the debris of unloved playthings of an age that had become digital was Justin and Kevin sharing the joint carefully, tenderly, both of them wanting to savour every drag. Between the latest of the plumes of smoke, Justin replied to what Kevin had been explaining. "Well, I'm glad you all like me." And, despite the lack of excitement, he was truthful in what he spoke – being accepted by the group meant a lot to him. As if shocked by what had been said, Kevin looked at him curiously.

"Really?"

"Well…" There was a momentary pause as Justin tried to work out how best to phrase how he was feeling. "I'm not really the sort of person that goes around seeking approval." A concession that the 23 year old agreed with without hesitation.

"Yeah, you don't seem the type."

"But still, they're good blokes, so I'm pleased they like me." Justin concluded, pleased that he managed to explain himself properly without causing offence to his newfound friendship.

Their unexpected catch up right now was more than enough to please Justin that all was going smoothly in him making something of his life, however frowned upon by certain false friends. But then it had gone one better when Kevin had stated, point blank, that the guys wanted Justin along for the ride to Manchester. After the other night, when Lloyd had caused the gang to pause and take stock of what must be done, he had hoped he would be given the chance to hold his own up north. Hooligan outbreaks at a football match were one thing, but travelling for a bender that was sure to go down in history was an opportunity he wanted in on. He wanted to defend the city that had given birth to him, even if it was a corrupt pool of filth that had done little to help him out in life.

"Fucking hell… really?"

"Yeah… *really*… we need a bloke like you, mate. You can hold your fucking own. Shit, in that game you were like a fucking monster." The last couple of words provoked a foolish grin from Justin as he sat and listened on tenterhooks, the promise of more adrenaline fuelled fun too much to handle. "You made most of them look like cunts."

Upon hearing that roundabout compliment, Justin burst out in a fit of laughter; not because of hearing how pathetic the other fans had been, but upon remembering the faces of each guy he'd gone for when the fight had gotten heavy and the police had been moving in. "I just wanted to fuck them up really." And that was the truth of it all; gone was the boy who stood along the sidelines and watched wanting to be part of the clique, now he was the clique and he could throw his weight around with the best of them. Or so he thought as he sat there feeling powerful whilst he smoked down the spliff.

"Yeah… you see that's the thing." *What's the 'thing'?* Justin couldn't help but think, finally allowing Kevin to be heard after

68

calming his torrent of self important thoughts. A 'thing' didn't sound good one bit, indeed it sounded like a massive 'but' was about to come along and mess up the plans Justin had immediately clung to like a child on Christmas Day. Seeing as a word hadn't been spoken to disturb him, Kevin pushed onward. "The lads, they're up for it, they really are. *But* they need to know whether you can really do it."

Even though he didn't want it to, and he tried to will it away, the fact that more was being demanded of him upset him no end. How could they even doubt him after everything he had done, after he had ended up with a couple of hours in the local cells thanks to tearing the pitch up at the Manchester vs London match? It seemed, to him, like a massive pile of bullshit, and one he wasn't about to take lying down. "You're having a fucking laugh right?! Didn't you see me fucking destroy it on Saturday?" Halfway through his second query, Kevin raised his hands in a mock surrender pose, though his face was thoroughly tickled by the outburst.

"Yeah, yeah I did. But it's not just enough to fucking beat a man, you've got to MARK a man."

"Mark a man?" He asked, a little uncomfortable about where the conversation was headed, but willing to plough along nonetheless.

"Yeah. To know that you don't give a shit, and you can go fucking beyond."

At that point Kevin had expected Justin to up and leave, insulted and bruised ego, but instead he sat there beside him and took the heat, and so far he hadn't shied away from it; this kid could go far if he kept it up. That he was certain of more than ever when Justin gave a begrudging "Fine".

"Really? Just like that?" Even Kevin had to profess that he was shocked.

"Yeah, just like that." What else could he have said? He didn't really want a part in this marking business because it sounded a lot more sinister than merely offloading some pent up tension and anger. But he figured that life was about challenges, of which he'd overcome many thus far, so why not add another to the list? "How do I do it?"

"Simple: we jump someone, and you leave a mark on his or her face."

"Fine. When?" His questions kept getting shorter and snappier as it became evident that there was no way he could avoid this gang initiation crap – hadn't the joke with the hooker been enough for them?

"We'll meet on Friday, and if it all goes well we'll be in Manchester by next week."

Cool. Doesn't sound so bad, no big deal. So why did he have a sinking feeling that he'd never experienced throughout the 18 years of his life so far? The smile that was plastered on his unblemished face spoke of excitement and eagerness, but his eyes betrayed him and revealed exactly what he felt, uncertainty. The smallest of glimmers but it was present all the same, and while Justin was confident Kevin hadn't spotted it, the 20 something had, and it delighted him to see the discord prowling around in Justin's head.

Chapter Ten

Getting headspace in a city full of bodies, all of which were looking for their lives to improve, and surrounded by concrete giants on every side, always proved difficult. There were a few parks throughout the jungle of roads and tube stations, but they did little to actually remove you from the hustle of the cosmopolitan. Parks, any patch of greenery for that matter, always drew the attention of people just like him looking to get away from the mundane grind of daily living. Everyone wanted their own shot at an oasis, but very few ever found one that could calm them like his haven did. It had taken a lot of time to find, and ironically it had always been in front of him, but it had been worth the searching. Here he could let go, and without the need to tear at flesh and lunge at another human.

Rooftops were always forgotten by people, unless they were looking to end their miserable existence, and therefore he was never disturbed, meaning that watching the sun rise was a moment all for himself. This was the closest he ever got to tranquility, and so he never shared the locale with others. Just as he was about to take in another deep lungful of air, coolness working down his throat as pleasurable as it was uncomfortable, a noise sounded from the door that led to the stairwell. Tainted by annoyance, tinged with shock, Justin spun round to look at who had dared to break the peace he had been feeling.

"Justin? What are you doing up here?" Danielle asked, her tone filled with concern. He guessed that he couldn't blame her realistically, as normal people tended not to head to the roof. Instead of reasoning about how quiet it was, and how it was the only time he got to himself, Justin responded regarding his name.

"Please don't call me that."

"What would you much rather... Jay?" She couldn't believe she was asking such a thing – being called Justin had never bothered him before, but then again *Jay* had never been so cold as he was right now. With a mumble of his preference, Danielle shook her head and wandered over to him, gently sitting herself beside her estranged childhood sweetheart.

In that moment, all she wanted to do was shake him to try and make him realise that the path he was going down with that group of thugs would be the undoing of him, but instead she traced the outline of his profile in her head. It wasn't that he didn't look the same anymore, but that he felt changed, like he was being moulded into a solider, only he had no purpose other than the whim of some wannabe. Sadness threatened to ooze from her every pore, but still she resisted, ever trying to save Justin's feelings at the expense of her own. Endeavouring to put her mental demons to rest, Danielle focused on the here and now, and more importantly why her idiotic friend was sat on the roof. "What are you doing here?"

"Knitting." He sniggered, though his reply was his usual sincere self, mixed in with a dash of sarcasm. "What does it look like I'm doing up here?"

"God, sometimes you're such a dickhead!" Danielle scorned, though she didn't feel annoyed in the slightest, for when Justin teased and played he was the boy she'd known for all those years, not the arsehole walking around with a grudge against anyone Kevin told him to. The trickle of his laughter warmed her no end.

Deep down she understood that Justin was not in control of this ridiculous journey he was on, even if he liked to think otherwise. And she also knew that he would eventually come to his senses and steer clear of the bullies he so hopelessly demanded respect from. The problem in all of it was the longevity of it all; too much time spent with pretenders would take him somewhere that would sully his name. Again, she cursed herself for being so easily drawn away from the briefest of moments with the same old Justin. "I can't remember the last time I was up here."

"I do it all the time, I fucking love it up here."

"What you thinking?" She pressed, unable to suppress her curiosity and worry any longer. Taken aback, and confused how they'd gone from reminiscing to interrogation, Justin frowned at her with immature annoyance.

"What do you mean?"

Friendship, lasting friendship, had various side benefits that came hand-in-hand with it, chiefly being able to anticipate and understand where the conversation was going. Danielle was aware of this just as much as he was, so he disliked how she was willing to pervert a window of calm for a chance to lecture him about his choices. *I just* know *that's what she's gonna bring up...*

"I can tell you're thinking something, so what is it?"

"Nothing." And as far as he was concerned right then, it was nothing. He didn't want to talk about it.

"It's about those fucking morons you're hanging out with, isn't it?"

"They're not morons." Were they? Justin wasn't so confident in his feelings anymore, not when they were so at war with one another about whether to mark or not mark some unknown. Growing up they'd heard about the perils of walking alone at night, and how dangerous gangs were in their need to brand you. It hadn't been silly back then to be scared, so why he felt compelled to tell himself it was stupid now was beyond him.

It was Danielle's turn to be annoyed. "They're fucking weekend warriors, Justin." What she had wanted to add was that they were on a crusade that had no meaning, no point, and were nothing but little boys swinging imaginary swords around in an attempt to win the age old contest of whose was bigger.

"They're about…"

"What?" Her voice raised slightly, passion getting the better of her. "Fighting? Fucking? That all sounds good, but what about when you're sixty and you can't see for shit?" A blistering gaze ensnared him as he tried to look away, the intensity of her conviction an aura so dense that no one could pierce it. In any other situation he would have admired her passion, but not here, and definitely not about this. This was off limits. "A lot of good all that stuff will be when you're older."

"You don't understand." Was the boy's weak reply, already knowing that she wouldn't drop this topic regardless of whether she did or didn't know things; Danielle was stubborn above all else.

"I think it's you that doesn't – there is more to life than that, you know."

Really? In all seriousness, was there more to life? Everyone was scrambling around looking for meaning that wasn't there, and they'd do it all sorts of ways, some were deemed good others bad. Why couldn't he just roll with what he wanted and deal with the consequences later? He was young, age was always on his side at this time in life, and if you couldn't gamble with that kind of favouritism then what was the point in ever being young. Nevertheless, he found himself quizzing her as to whether 'more' even existed. "Really?"

"Yes. Really." Danielle replied, hoping that she'd broken through his pigheaded behaviour. However, when he stood up and refused to look her way, she realised that it had all been in vain; Justin didn't want to search for more when he already believed he had it with Kevin and his questionable company.

"Well, when you see it look me up, yeah?" To say he was tired of their pep talk was an understatement.

"Where are you going?"

"Anywhere but here." *Away from you.*

What she wanted to do was stand, to grab hold of him and shake him until his eyeballs rolled back in their sockets, but she simply didn't have the strength to stand. It hurt so much to hear him so disillusioned about the world, and while she could understand given his home life, that didn't automatically mean she should give up. There was always something to fight for, just sometimes you had to dig deeper to discover it. "Justin!" Her cry shot across the growing distance between them like a bullet in the night, and it hit him in the back, somewhere close to his heart. It was a moment, nothing more, but he looked her way again anyway.

"It's not Justin, it's Jay." So monotonous was his tone, so robotic and unfeeling, like a drone. The need to say something was extraordinarily painful it almost felt like it would rip open her chest, but she couldn't do or say anything. That glimpse of the boy she had loved, and still did? It had just been burnt up by another that had snatched his body and assumed his identity.

Although he about turned swiftly, he had seen the expression of despair that had clawed its way across her naturally beautiful face. The anguish Danielle was feeling because of him was far worse than any blemish he could leave upon another, indeed if he had watched anyone else do this to a friend he'd have stepped in and given them a piece of his mind. Yet he wasn't about to do that, instead he would walk away and listen to her gentle sobs.

***

The day had denied a quick transition into night after that encounter, almost as if the passage of time wanted to make Justin relive every word spoken between Danielle and himself. He had always known that time was cruel, but this felt personal – but was it just nerves eating at him and derailing his sensibilities? When the night had tapped on his bedroom window and instructed him to dress for an outing that was only known between him and fellow conspirators, he had strived to distract himself with video games. They hadn't worked, mainly because in each title he owned, some kind of kill came into play and it in turn caused the ball of nerves bouncing around his stomach to grow bigger.

As if to signal his oncoming death of the self he and everyone else knew, a flash of light twinkled through the gap in his curtains, and as much as he'd tried to put it down to passing headlights, he knew exactly what it meant. The time was now for him to make his mark. Even in spite of knowing that, of not needing to cross from his bed and peer out the window, he did so anyway, as if on the off chance he'd been mistaken. Below on the street, their grins white in the depths of the stormy blue sky, stood the lads, all ready to see Jay finally be born. A smile instinctively pulled at his mouth, yet he didn't feel the warmth of it like he had thought he would.

Chapter Eleven

The estate looked quite peaceful at night, well, as peaceful as it could given its geographical location and the backgrounds of most of its inhabitants. And they were about to destroy the calm; they were an oncoming storm to some poor unsuspecting individual who were probably late home after a bad day at work. Still, for now they were just a group of men laughing and joking their way to their destination, not a single care in the world to any of their names. For tonight's entertainment it was Milton who was up for a roasting, the others doubtful about his latest sexual conquest and her apparent beauty. "I'm telling you, she was fit!" He exclaimed, mildly antagonised by how easily they disregarded the slightest notion that he may have bedded an attractive woman.

It had been that way since he had found the men and become part of their crew: he would give details about his latest shag, and they would all laugh themselves stupid in saying she'd been ugly or a man. Tonight was the latter of the two. "Really? Was she able to tuck her cock out of the way then?" Lloyd jested, thoroughly amused that Milton looked so exasperated. Impressed by the ferocity of his tease, the remaining men of the herd chortled along with Lloyd.

"Yeah, yeah, you're all fucking hilarious." Came the grumbled response, the joke not so funny when he was the butt of it, a factor that made everyone else roar all the louder. In attempt to ease any ill feelings, Frankie had extended a faux apology.

"It's not that we don't believe you, Milton."

"It's just we know you'd fuck anything." Boomed George, spittle foaming at the corners of his mouth from excessively trying not to laugh right in Milton's face.

Justin laughed and grinned along with them, delighted in the banter that they exchanged. Too often the word 'banter' was associated with being a jerk, a man who poked fun at the expense of others, and yet he had only ever seen it as a fun time amongst friends. It was a universal form of communication that the majority didn't mind, provided they didn't all have sticks up their backsides.

Now it was Kevin's turn to prod a weary looking Milton, who despite appreciating the good fun of it all, looked like he was ready to glass anyone of them in the face. "So the last thing you will fuck would be a good looking bird?"

"Bollocks to you."

"Maybe she had three tits like the chick in *Total Recall*." Lloyd added.

"More like three cocks." Frankie deduced, his eyes glittering with mischief and amusement; he was enjoying this no end, probably more than the others were. Even though he had to admit that he was relishing this topic a lot more than usual, or indeed the others, the comforting laughter of everyone else reassured him that he was okay to use Milton as a verbal punching bag.

However, when they stepped into the mouth of a long and rather smelly alleyway, Kevin raised his hands to still their merriment, and a hush descended over them with ungodly speed. Nobody needed to hear that they were where they needed to be tonight. Each one of them turned to look at Justin, those beastly grimaces back on their smug faces once more. In that moment, when faced with the toothy grin of the pack, Justin couldn't help but feel he was making the biggest mistake of his life. What made matters worse for him was that he knew he couldn't run from it now, if he did, he'd lose the pack and lose the respect he'd steadily been building.

The waiting was the worst part, and as he cast his eyes yet again over the tunnel before him, Justin couldn't help but think that anyone who graced this part of the estate deserved to be beaten. Anything to help calm his doubts. Alleyways weren't nice at the best of times, when daylight penetrated their enclosed dimensions, but at night, when the darkness clung to every single corner, they became something a lot more unpleasant. Only the arrogantly brave and the desperately stupid would even think to venture down there, shortcut or no. Maybe if he kept thinking like that it would make marking someone that little bit easier…

"You know this spot?" Kevin quizzed, watching Justin investigate the length of the sideway avenue once more.

"Fucking hell, definitely."

"This is the spot."

Although he wasn't going to question why or risk the disapproving looks and jibes of the more experienced members, he didn't get why they wanted to select somewhere so close to home. It seemed completely stupid to risk being caught red handed, with their homes little more than a mile away, though maybe that was the point of it all – to be caught; Justin hoped not. A football match telling off was nothing in comparison to being arrested for marking someone, a person you didn't even have any ill will towards. His stomach lurched savagely. "What do you mean?" There was no need to ask, but he couldn't stop himself from asking it nevertheless.

"Your target is going to come down here." Kevin gave a look that said that that much was obvious, and that pussying out now wasn't an option that would go well for Justin. Transparent or not, Justin needed more, though he wasn't sure what that missing something actually was.

"What did he do?" A shrug was all that greeted his next question, and that was even worse. He was totally fine messing up someone that deserved it, at least in principle anyway, after all, didn't bad people get what was coming to them? But to target a randomer, with no real impact on their lives, now that seemed unreasonable and barbaric even to him and his budding love for violence. "I don't understand – I thought we was going to do over a rival, you know, a proper vile cunt." The bellowing sounds that weighed down on him was infuriating; they were making fun of him, he was the next Milton on their piss take list.

A truth that Milton all too readily stepped up to and threw in the insults before anyone else, saying he was overeager would have been a compliment. "He's like a babe in the fucking woods." Milton quipped, sheer glee radiating off of him, something that the others absorbed and used as their own.

"Fuck off, Milton." Justin couldn't stand it, he wasn't there to be made fun of, and even though the lads would likely claim the banter card if he protested he knew that this wasn't banter, it was a dressing down that was designed to humiliate. He didn't want to succumb to it, but he doubted he'd challenge it given where he was, and all the people currently stationed around him. He would take the place of the victim if someone else didn't, if he behaved like that towards them.

"What would be the point in that?" Kevin suggested in answer to Justin's previous innocent enquiry.

"Kev... *everyone* uses this alleyway."

"Yeah, and you're going to make your mark on the first bastard that comes through."

"But they might be—"

"What?" Kevin shot back, loathing coating his words. "Innocent? Sweet? Then let's fucking hope so. Beating up some vile cunt at a footy game, that's fucking easy, but for me to know, truly know, you have my back... If you're willing to take out anyone..."

Justin looked down the alleyway once more, a creeping sensation clutched to his spine and clawing its way up to his head, every inch a painful thrill of fresh fear. He was trying to think it through, to be calm and collected about it all: he didn't know the person from Adam, so why did it matter in the long run. Sure, someone would be hurt that didn't deserve it, but that was how the world worked whether he danced to the same tune or not. And while he could fight against the grain of humanity and try to be a crusader of compassion and pacifism, it was unlikely anyone else would pay that courtesy to him if he he had been the intended victim. It really was a dog eat dog world, and he was damned if he was about to be eaten.

As if on cue to reaffirm that sentiment, Kevin cut through his thoughts – "Remember, Jay, I will never ever tell you what to do. But if you don't do this, then you'll lose a lot of fucking respect." Justin turned back to look at them, a last ditch attempt at gauging whether approval was worth the hassle or not. "So what's it going to fucking be?" There was no escaping it any longer, for none of them were going to allow more stalling, it was now or never on whether he wanted to be in with them or not. But the idea of losing the family he'd just found, of the people who readily accepted him, was too great to ignore, and so Justin smiled in response. Though his facial muscles twitched into an arrogant smirk, inside dread was setting in and pooling in the depth of his body.

***

Hours ticked by and the shades of night made their way from navy to black with each 60 minute interval, as if it was helping to hide the terror Justin was waiting to unleash. Not that it comforted him whether anyone was on his side or not, for he was the one about to smear someone across the sides of the passage. The thought made him shudder. "I know what you're thinking." whispered Kevin, noting that the shudder that had just seized Justin's body had nothing to do with the chill of the air. Curious, Justin pressed the man further.

"You do?"

"Yeah. You're wondering if I had to do this, and the answer is yes I did."

Hearing that someone else had been in this exact position shouldn't have pleased the lad so, but it did, and morals could be damned. If Kevin was able to do this and live through it unblemished, clearly not stained by the disgrace of such an act, then why couldn't Justin do the same; they were no different from one another.

"An alley?"

"No, mine was somewhere else, some poor bastard in a supermarket car park." Remorse was thick and sticky as it dripped from Kevin's downturned mouth, a small but powerful way of him showing that Justin needn't worry that he was alone in his experience.

"Why though?"

"Because he was there." And the remorse, that glimpse that the man he held in such high regard actually functioned like a normal human being, was gone as quick as it had appeared. Now it was back to business.

Justin was about to comment that he doubted anyone was even going to come by they'd waited so long, when from somewhere further down the alley Lloyd hissed that someone was coming. It was showtime. Hoping against hope that the 30 year old was wrong, Justin looked up with them, but sure enough a silhouette was moving down the man-made corridor towards them. Although no features could be distinguished from this far away, they all could make out a briefcase hung by the man's side. *He's just a normal guy...* Justin argued to himself as he observed the purposeful stride that the man possessed; he was clearly a man that felt good about his life and what he was achieving with it. Although it wasn't necessary, Kevin said "There he is."

"I'm not sure." The teenager shot back, the nerves he'd been repressing now breaking his voice.

"It's your fucking choice, *Justin*, but remember what I said about respect." Even though he wasn't about to get into it now,

Justin hated how Kevin played around with his name whenever he wanted to make a point. If the boy was good it was Jay, but if the other ventured to disobey he was back to Justin, his gay name.

Looking back towards the intended target, Justin was absentmindedly aware of Milton slipping a bottle into the boy's empty hand. Surprisingly, even to himself, he gripped it with firm conviction: he would do this. "It's now or never." Someone breathed, delirium of their frenzy not far away. Sucking in the air to steady himself, Justin stepped in front of the target, an abrupt movement that had taken the businessman by complete surprise. For a second there was a locking of eyes, although the exchange was unclear and without focus, and then, without any more hesitation, Justin raised the bottle above his head and brought it crashing down onto the victim. Shortly followed by a howling scream that vibrated through all of them and the surrounding buildings.

Working off pure adrenaline now, Justin flew into action, yelling with every kick and punch he landed, his feet relentlessly stamping on the crumpled man below. Foolish although it was to even try, the man curled into the fetal position to cushion himself from the blows, a pitiful display that spurred Justin on all the more. The coward couldn't even take the beating like a man, he had to hide his body in a ball and lay there like a child. Again. Again. Again, his feet crushed downwards, but then… then he saw it… that watch. He knew that watch. It was fancy, it was expensive, it had been saved for from hard earned cash of being a respectable man with a career. It was Eddie's watch.

And sure enough, when he stopped briefly to look at the target's face for the first time since he'd jumped him, he saw to his horror that it was indeed Ed that he was beating on. "The fuck?!" He cried out, unable to hold back his confusion.

"Go on lads!" Milton screamed into the air, the lads all charging towards Justin and Eddie, their sights firmly set on bringing pain.

He couldn't though, how could he now that he knew? Justin stumbled backwards, his whole being fixated on Eddie who was now receiving far worse a beating than what Justin had just been dishing out, and he had been going at it full pelt. The gang was awesome in their terror. One member though wasn't quite all in yet, and that was Kevin, who offered a smile at Justin that reeked of hostility and perverse pleasure; it contorted his face into that of a devil. So caught up on that malice, Justin hadn't even noticed that the cries had stopped, but Eddie was still now, thankfully taken away from consciousness to spare him of more waking agony. The quiet caused the men to stop and step away, all of them facing their little lamb. "He's all yours." Kevin murmured, a devilish leer piercing through the dim night.

More to see if he was going to pull through than anything else, Justin gingerly walked over to Eddie, his friend a sorry state of blood, spit, bruises, and sweat. *It shouldn't have been him*, he thought sorrowfully, unable to forget all the times his wise friend had been there for him, through thick and thin. It didn't matter that they'd fought, friends did that, what mattered was that he was going to be okay. The anger built as he called back to Kevin. "You knew?"

"Of course I fucking knew."

"You fucking…" Justin mumbled, struggling to hold back tears that had been waiting all too long to fall.

"Make your mark."

"If I had known…"

"Known what, known it was him? Yeah right. You're still going to make your mark. Then you really will be one of us." Milton, followed by Kevin, chanted to 'make it', a childish egging on that would have usually thrilled Justin. But not now, not when Eddie was a growing stain on the pavement.

As if sensing that their babe would carry it out, even though he didn't want to, all of them stepped back, an expectant and hungry audience demanding that the climax begin. They'd waited long enough. Standing over him Justin undid his zipper, disgusted that he was even about to do it, and yet he didn't even attempt to stop himself. What was the point? He'd come this far, and he'd let them kick Eddie into a pulp, what difference would the mark make now. A stream of urine quickly followed, causing everyone to break out into celebration, all except Justin, who simply continued to alleviate his bladder, misery clinging to him.

Chapter Twelve

That night had taken some time to forget, and if truth be told, he still hadn't managed to wash the disgrace and shame away. He'd tried the moment he had gone home; the shower had been several degrees too high, and the stream of beaded water had scolded his flesh as he had stood there and cried. Anger and sadness had come together to create a heady formula that no man, no matter how masculine, was immune to. The fact that he hadn't stayed to watch over Eddie had also been another branch of the intense guilt he was now carrying. After he'd zipped up and bowed his head, the guys led by Kevin, were all eager to run off and honour the occasion elsewhere. Not that he had asked for them to help Eddie, or even to be kind enough to call an ambulance (like they even would have), but he still felt bad that he'd left his friend there lying in the piss and dirt.

Not bad enough not to come along though, eh, Jay? He mocked himself, his vision rolling over the whizzing scenery that kept rushing past the coach window. Although it was madness to do so, Justin had been at the Manchester minibus meeting point all the same, geared up and ready (more than ready) for a weekend bender that would flush out the last images of poor Eddie.

The minivan was for them alone and still it managed to sound like a whole arena was back there beside him, such was their singalongs and cheers. He supposed it was good that they were enjoying themselves, even if he wasn't. Despite having his eyes on the road, Kevin couldn't avoid the gut wrenching forlorn state of Justin seated next to him, the pathetic specimen making him seethe. What he wanted to do was slam the brakes, pull the mardy dickhead from the seat, and give him exactly what Eddie had gotten. What he actually did was turn to him with feigned concern. "What's got you so down in the dumps?" Even though the question was dressed up to look innocent, Justin knew better, and the fact that Kevin even had the nerve to play so dumb ticked him off no end. How could he sit there and not understand how distressing it had been for Justin? He'd had to beat up and piss on his friend for fuck's sake!

"You fucking know – you fucking tricked me!"

"And?" The driver replied, thirsty to see how gutsy his apprentice could be. Kevin wanted him to rage, to throw caution to the wind, to challenge him, but he knew he'd never do any of that because he didn't have the balls. Justin was a good guy but he was a pleaser, and yes men like that rarely left their comfort zones unless there was no other choice, like the alleyway.

In the back seats sat oblivious faces too jumped up on their roadtrip to care that the conversation in the front sounded a little prickly. Besides, if it got too out of hand they'd just pull over and dump Justin, it was no big deal for them, one less member to throw at the Manchester gangs wouldn't make that much of a difference. Fodder was always good to have, but they'd manage. Nonetheless, Frankie couldn't help but lift his head their way when he faintly heard Justin moan that Kevin had known all along it was Eddie who was the target.

Back in the front, unaware that they had been drawing attention from at least one of the group, the pair continued to lock horns. "Of course I fucking knew! But you still didn't have a problem pissing on his head did you?" He spat, fired up at having to point out that Justin acted of his own accord, not one of them ever forcing him to take his cock out and piss all over the guy.

"Yeah right… Like you would've let me not do that."

"Look, to be part of the crew we have to know how far you will take it. How far you're willing to go."

"And that was the bloody test?" Justin quipped back, unable to believe that somebody was so desperate to test loyalty that they'd get someone to attack a complete innocent, to him that logic was no better than 'just because'. A word wasn't uttered by the other, though his hands appeared to grip the steering wheel a little tighter while he envisioned straggling Justin. "The bloke in the supermarket? You knew him didn't you?"

The smile that had awaited that response had sickened him, and in his repulsion he had left the topic there, dead and buried, all too eager to focus back on the road than listen to more thuggish bullshit. This was the life he was leading, and although it was exhilarating at times, the fact that it scared him so much made him wonder whether it was too late to walk away. Gathering by how pressurised he'd been to mark Eddie, he guessed that he already had his answer.

Out of the window a sign for 'MANCHESTER' loomed. They were close.

***

As the hooligans and their minibus full of menace raced towards the northern city, back in London was the mess that Justin had left behind; Eddie was a battered and swollen mess. It pained her to see him like this, a man that had always gone out of his way to help people, and never judged whilst doing so. Even having come from the same background as herself and Justin, even after getting in with a lot similar to Kevin's, Eddie had managed to come back time and time again, proving everyone wrong about council estates and its families.

Gently she reached out and clutched his hand tightly, hoping that her sleeping friend would soon be back among the conscious. A single tear leaked out and tumbled down Danielle's already grubby tear stained cheeks; how at a time like this, when Eddie needed him most, could Justin be on a trip to bloody

Manchester! It amazed her how heartless he'd become, *how much like Kevin he'd become.* And try as she might, she couldn't push away the feeling that Justin had been involved with this somehow, though she couldn't understand why he'd do such a thing if it were true.

***

When they had pulled up in Manchester, the mood had decidedly changed: Justin had been given other things to focus on, and therefore the guys hadn't needed to worry about him having a moral episode while away with them.

They strutted like kings through the streets of the cultural metropolis, larking around like naughty kids on a daytrip rather than grown men, something which irked various passersby. Not that they went out of their way to comment on the behaviour, for they'd already seen them get up in someone's face for remarking on how loud they were being. Nobody had time to be harassed when it was easier to ignore the problem and move on. Currently they had no destination in mind, it was just a case of walking around getting loud and leery and seeing which crew they antagonised first. Oh, how Justin craved the hum of a roughhouse right about now, to knock the pearly teeth of some preteneious arsehold who'd had it coming for most of his life – *Like Eddie did, hm?* God, how he hated that his mind had the ability to suck the joy out of the few pleasures he had left.

Their first showdown had taken place in a carpark that only the very desperate used, for lingering there too long, alone, was ill advised. Anyone that tried it had often returned to a smashed up vehicle emptied of their belongings, or had been quickly dragged off and abused in such a manner that they'd not spoken about it to a soul in years. Such dejected places were ideal for men like them, like *him.* They could work out their issues on someone who warranted it.

Although there had been quite a few men to choose from to square up to, it had been the largest of the bunch that Justin had made a beeline for, much to the amusement of the others who assumed that he must either be ready to unleash a side they hadn't seen, or was itching to be killed. Either way the show would be an intriguing one, and one they were sure they'd walk away from at the very least. Funnily enough though, they had been watching on and off between attacks now, and so far Justin had been incredible – he'd torn and growled like the wild animal he was when the mood took hold of him. And he had gone several rounds before Kevin finally intervened, from behind with a mighty swing of a baseball bat that made the sickest of crunching sounds as it destroyed the skull like wet tissue.

Once the ogre was slain and the men could relax for a second, Kevin sounded their victory and pointed them in the direction of a nearby club he'd heard rave reviews about. Why should they just go large on the gangs when they could have a lot of action between the sheets as well. Not to mention that it was about time that Jay got his end away and fucked like the man he wanted to be, not sniffing around some council estate girl who wasn't worth shit in comparison to the babes that should be on his arm.

***

As clubs went it was pretty much the same old: loud music, lots of swaying bodies, sex outside and fingering on the dancefloor, exactly what you'd expect from an establishment such as this on a weekend. Put side by side against the London clubs, the lads had to hand it to Manchester and their nightlife scene as they'd got it right as far as they were concerned. Even though they had every intention of hitting the dancefloor, for now they remained by the bar, indulging in some much needed relaxation; their muscles were aching, and the cuts from their earlier fights had now come to the surface in the full glory of pink and red. Accompanied by their wounds of a good time, they joked while knocking back shot after shot, Justin only outdone by Kevin.

"Say this for them, they know how to do a fucking good nightclub!" Boomed Milton, a ruddy rosetta shade spreading across his cheeks and to the tip of his nose.

"I know!" Agreed Lloyd who, despite the lack of colour, was actually slurring far worse than anyone else.

Kevin however, had other intentions. While the scene was all well and good, and the thump of the tempo coursing through his veins was pleasant, it was the girls further down the bar looking over at Justin and himself that currently held his interest. Or at least the lower half of his interest. Certain that Jay had yet to catch on, he leaned closer to the boy and bellowed that they were in if he was game. As the girls grinned at them they smirked back, and an unwritten exchange took place that said all four of them were going to get lucky tonight. Sadly though, not everyone shared such good feelings about the inevitable tryst that was going to be taking place later, and that everyone was actually a someone, and that someone was Milton. Unhappy by being overlooked by women he was damn sure would beg for more after a few minutes with him, he eyed up the dancefloor and made a split second decision to let loose over there. "Fuck this, I'm going to dance!"

As bad as the jokes had been surrounding Milton before, they were nothing compared to how they would be after witnessing that 'exhibit'. Even though it was refreshing to see someone so intoxicated by the flow of the music, it was equally hilarious to watch his body go through the motions that looked more like the beginnings of a heart attack rather than a dance of passion. If he had been about to pull, they mused, he definitely wouldn't now. As he observed through fits of giggles, Justin couldn't help but return to his old way of thinking about the group he was part of – they weren't always nice, but they had each other's backs, and that was the main thing. Too often good people screwed over their loved ones, but not these guys, they shared something a lot deeper than love, and more strong than hate: bloodlust. An uncontrollable desire that bonded them.

"FUCK SAKE!"

The sound of the shout, and the anger that flooded from it, drew Justin's attention: Milton had, completely unintentionally, knocked a pint out of a guy's hand. It wasn't a major offense, but it was evident that the guy whose drink was now being trampled under the weight of sticky heels, felt differently. He was a large fella, and he looked like there was no way that a simple 'sorry' was going to be acceptable. Unheeding of the harm glaring him in the face, Milton shrugged an apology partnered up with a drunken smile, and resumed his flailing dance… right up until the man grabbed Milton and threw him across the dancefloor.

The sudden uncalled for behaviour had them all springing into action, flocking to the floor and to Milton's aid. On cue, and as if by magic, several men who had remained unseen thus far immediately joined the larger man and created a wall of bodies, a cliche us vs them set up that had the crowd looking on with a mix of emotions that primarily ran off excitement. "Fucking come on then you wankers!" roared Milton's attacker, all cocksure of himself and his cronies, much to the annoyance of Justin who was readying his fists to land a perfect wallop straight between the eyes. Before he'd even raised his whitening knuckles, Kevin had tapped his hand away and strided between them, a move that was altogether out of character. Turned to the boys having dared to chance a loss of contact between him and the rival gang, Kevin instructed for them to retreat.

"You fucking what?!" Screamed George, his eyes darting from Milton to the head Manc and then back again, as if that was all the evidence Kevin needed.

"Fucking leave it!" He repeated, though this time there was an edge to his speech that challenged someone to defy him, to ignore his final word and charge in; if they did that, they'd have him to worry about, not the Manchester hooligan leering behind him.

Filled with what was three quarters shame and one total and utter shock, the boys parted to allow Kevin to pass through, before filing one by one after him. While it was a pitiful sight for them to be part of, the better part of the clubbers had already lost interest and were partying like normal, but not that other group, no, they watched with vindictive euphoria. "That's right you fucking wankers, you just walk away!" That taunt, while not nearly as brutal as the ones uttered only minutes ago, caught Kevin's attention and made him turn back to survey the headman one last time. His reward? Getting the middle finger, and still he merely walked away, his head held high but surrendering nonetheless, it was maddening to Justin and his mates.

Last to the table, he received the iciest of receptions, with Milton the most frosty about what had just happened. "What the fuck, Kevin?! You made us look like a bunch of fucking cunts!" Although nobody rushed to agree with Milton, they all knew he had a valid and blindingly striking point. After travelling all this way, with the sole intention to fuck things up, it made absolutely no sense to them that Kevin would turn down a fight. Surely not the man who had only claimed a matter of days before that he was a 'nutcase'.

"We're here to get fucking drunk, not get into a rumble all the fucking time!"

"Oh for fuck's sake!" came the protest before Kevin turned his back and locked onto Jay, his sights now back on the beautiful women that were still admiring them both from the safety of the bar.

"Seriously though, what was that about?" continued George, not happy to not know exactly why they'd be ordered to stand down and sit on the naughty step like little children. Kevin rolled his eyes to the heavens, peeved that not only did he have to repeat himself again, but that he was distracted from the throbbing bulge growing in his boxers.

"Like I said," He emphasised. "It's about having a good fucking time." What the rest of that sentence really said was 'back the fuck off and shut the hell up'.

Finally able to return to their conquests at hand, Kevin and Justin looked at the girls in unison before looking at one another, both of them sporting a twinkle in their eyes. "So, Jay, where were we?"

"I don't know, but I know where I wanna be!"

Chapter Thirteen

Moans echoed around the room with each thrust of his hips, her body arching with pleasure, the beads of sweat only adding to her allure and sex appeal. And that body, oh it was truly breathtaking to watch as she writhed and squirmed, the tightness of her sending him into spasms of rapture as she enveloped him, taking in every inch. He'd seen sex like this before, had masturbated to it on numerous occasions, but to be in the moment for real, to feel something so wet and tight, that would take some beating.

On the way over to her flat he had worried about his nerves, and the drink if he had been fully honest; nervous because he wasn't a serial player and therefore hadn't racked up much experience, and the drink because he didn't want to lose his erection midway through. Even more so with Kevin plying away in the back room, ensuring that Justin had a constant competition on his hands to please his girl that little bit more. At first it had been a horrible thought, after all who wants to hear their mate have sex, but then he'd relaxed when he'd noticed that he was just as good if not more so when it came to making a girl cum. And oh how she came. It was amazing, and although he kept his pride in check, he couldn't help but fuck her with a heightened level of confidence each time she fell apart in front of him, her breathy cries for more a sound of pure victory.

Again she came, this time so hard that she clawed down his back, causing him to gasp slightly, the touch so raw and yet so gratifying. Spent up for the night, and probably for the rest of the week, Justin allowed himself and the girl to part, his female companion choosing to rollover and nod off into a world of sleep while he grasped at a towel discarded on the ground and crept into the living room. It wasn't that he didn't want to stick around, it was more that he needed to stretch his legs and get some fresh air that didn't smell of sex. As the door provided its telltale *click* Kevin looked up and beckoned for Jay to join him for a joint; it was well earned all things considered.

"Feeling better?" He asked casually, his body relaxed after what felt like a lifetime of tension.

"What do you think?" He smirked back, his eyes looking over to the door and then back to the glowing tip of the smoke.

"What is she doing?"

"Sleeping." It was Kevin who grinned now, happy to see that Justin was ridding himself of societal restricts and savouring life as it came, quite literally.

"Well, with a seeing to like that…"

Right now he could say anything: 'yeah, I'm good', 'hot damn what a lay', and all manners of terribly cliche and unnecessary smug hints at being some kind of stud. Instead however, he chose to remain quiet, happy in the knowledge that it was bloody good for him and it sounded great for her. Not even the worry of whether she faked it entered his mind, for if she had, more fool her, he'd had fun and that was ultimately what mattered in the rules of engagement for this one night stand.

"Where's yours?" Justin eventually asked, almost having forgotten that he'd been boning in sync with his friend and leader for most of the night. He followed Kevin's thumb as he pointed to the sofa on which was sprawled out a deeply unconscious girl, the alcohol having won this round with ease; a troubling sight for Justin. "Was she even conscious?"

"Whatever." had been the response he had been fearing, if not the one he would be most surprised about. The girl had been pretty wasted on the brief walk home, but it had seemed like she'd been more than awake when Justin had waved goodbye and gone to play the field in the other room. Now though, in the lamplight of the street shining through the window cracks, he couldn't help but look at the woman as a victim. Justin hoped he was wrong.

Undeterred by abrupt change in the boy's body language, Kevin laughed lightly before signalling for the seat to be filled beside him. Without no more than muffled footsteps and the creak of the chair, Justin placed himself down and took the joint, appreciating the distinct taste of the grass that had been scored. "Fuuuuuck, that's strong."

"Totally worth it though." Was reasoned as they exchanged the smoldering stick of tobacco between them.

"The lads will be proper fucked off you know." Justin stated, unable to resist the growing white elephant in the room any longer. When they had left the nightclub, all the lads had looked disgruntled and ready to jump Kevin, so it seemed likely that they would harbour ill feelings after being given a night to nurture their ire. Shockingly, Kevin *did* appreciate what was being said to him.

"I know, you know."

"Then why did you…?"

As his companion shifted next to him, Justin mistook the movement for discomfort, and decided that now wasn't the time, and it was best to move on and maybe ask at a later date. But when Kevin's arm came protruding in front of his face heralding a scar that looked as angry as the day it had been given, Justin recognised that there was more to what had happened tonight than he'd first thought. "His name is Jack. He's a local hooligan who is the head of the toughest Manchester gang." He motioned for Jay to look closely at every dent and gnarled mound of skin that had healed since the encounter, and it was a sight that Justin would never forget. "The cunt gave me this on the last away game."

"Fuuuuck, that's nasty!"

"Yup, and I want some fucking payback." He snarled under his breath as he rolled his sleeve down and over the mark, the brand returned to its hiding place.

"Is that why, is that why we're here?" Although it wasn't necessary to ask or to be heard, Justin thought it would do some good to get every fact and tiny detail out into the open, and not just for his own benefit of understanding the type of man that Jack was. It also allowed Kevin to lift a weight off of himself that had clearly been ladened on him since he was last in this city.

In spite of how he'd felt about the girls being asleep earlier, he was now grateful for it as they didn't pose any kind of distraction to either of them. If they had been awake and fawning all over them, purring for attention and wanting, neither would have easily resisted and understandably so. But now that they were subdued and out of the picture, removed from the game so to speak, Justin could coax out of Kevin what his overall plan was for getting revenge. He had already guessed that with a target as infamous as Jack that they'd have to plan quickly and thoroughly, ensuring that his friends didn't get wind and turn up to balls up the whole operation. One thing that ate away at Jay though was why there'd been such a wait for this time to come – Kevin wasn't normally a patient man, so what had made him tow the line in this way? "Why didn't you get him in London?" He enquired, his voice peppered with tangible curiosity grown into confusion.

"Was fucking told I couldn't."

As far as revelations went, this one was significant for Justin to hear. His friend, his idol, and more notably the chief of the group, had actually listened to someone else and kept his urges in check, even though it had directly clashed with what he wanted. It made sense why Justin's mark had been so important to the man now, for it was like looking in a mirror and seeing if anyone else had a character such as his: to be able to look in the face of something you don't want to do and continue to do it anyway.

Justin still didn't like what had happened, and he doubted he ever would, but he could now discern that it hadn't been all about an organised attack against Eddie. To say it made him feel a little at ease wasn't exactly true, but he couldn't deny that knowing they shared common experiences made him reassess his feelings about Kevin. What had recently been soured had now been righted, in a way. Not that it meant he wouldn't question the who and why the lads had had to stand down. "What? By who?"

"I deal a bit on the side, my employer seems to think it would cause too much agro." A sentiment that it was apparent he didn't share.

"You're going to…?"

In all honesty, he wasn't sure what he was trying to ask as there wasn't a lot of maneuver room for Kevin to work with; he was damned if he behaved and he was most certainly in for a world of shit if he defied his employer. Justin had surmised that while he knew nothing about the man pulling the strings, he sorely doubted that he would be any friendlier than his scarred comrade, ergo, nothing positive would happen as a result of disobedience. All the same, the employer was someone he needed to have a grasp of if nothing else – if he was to be a puppet or another pawn then he wanted to know the puppeteer.

Although it had taken him some time to respond, Kevin eventually shared his eloquent views on the whole affair, in his usual poetic and dignified repose: "Fuck them. I don't give a shit about rules." *Really? Says the man who has listened to them so far…* "People like you and I? We don't follow fucking rules." A character review that Justin wasn't overly fond of because both of them *had* been following all sorts of guidelines up until this point. So if anything, they were opting to deviate from their normal habits after a period of avid devotion.

"Even so, this might cause all sorts of shit." Jay worried aloud, the restless feelings he put to bed earlier now back at the surface, bubbling, again.

"Then bring it fucking on, I say!" Spoken like a true warrior, something that they were both sceptical to call Kevin in spite of his past exploits, not that either would admit that to the other as they preferred ignorance to honesty in a world of deceit such as theirs. Justin couldn't help but sigh deeply, *their world... that's what it was now... No me and them, just us. Theirs. Ours.* He wasn't sure why the notion unsettled him, but it did all the same.

"Do the lads know?"

"Of course not."

A secret told only to him was another warning signal he'd have preferred to avoid. While having a confidante and vice versa was always a lovely thing for people to have, when information as sensitive as this was passed along to an underling (which he evidently was in the grand scheme of things), it wasn't a healthy sign. "But why tell me?" His delicate voice implored, the seriousness of the matter quietening his tones to that of a child. "Because I trust you," Came Kevin's reply. "We're one in the same – from the same neighbourhood, the same background." That then was the first time that he'd ever thought about how similar they were, when all the bravado was peeled away, and his chief was scrutinised as little more than the flesh and bones he was, then it wasn't hard at all to see how they matched one another like bookends. "Is that why you wanted me in the crew?" *So you weren't alone?*

Kevin's corners of his lips twitched, a beginning of a knowing smile that didn't quite make it to its final form. "You know one day, you'll have your own crew, taking names and fucking cunts up."

"My own crew?" Justin stuttered, surprised by the faith that was placed in him. The disbelief hadn't fallen on deaf ears, and Kevin frowned when he next spoke.

"Fucking hell, yeah! You would be a legend, mate. The way you fight? You're like a fucking demon." Nothing like an ego stroke to build character, though Justin was sure his head would be too big for the door if Kevin kept laying it on so thick.

"I learned from the best."

"Yeah? Who was that?" Although he suspected that his friend wasn't looking for cheesy praise that was ultimately a lie, Justin still felt guilty that he wasn't about to say Kevin's own name back to him.

"My dad."

As eyes widened and realisation set it, followed by unsaid respect for a man that he'd never known, both Kev and Justin sat in the pale light and toked their joint, the undisturbed silence of the moment savoured for it felt like it could be the last in a long time.

Chapter Fourteen

After they had finished their post coital roll up, the men had very quietly dressed, nodded the sleeping ladies a bid farewell, and then vacated the building in all the glory of a typical walk of shame. It wasn't that they didn't want to chat with them, it was more that they both wanted to avoid any awkwardness that was due to follow once beer goggles had slipped off and harsh light of day highlighted every blemish. Their stroll back to the hotel had been a brief one, and with the majority of the others out for the count nursing the beginnings of monster hangovers, explaining away the events of the night had proven easy. Justin and Kevin had shared a rare moment, and it had shaped their relationship, for the better in the 18 year old's naive eyes.

Now the semi-decent bedroom was long gone and a grotty backstreet pub that would sooner cut a newcomer than let them in was their current haunt. Well, the area outside it was anyway. There they waited and watched, the thump of their hearts beating perfectly in time to a racing beat that sounded like it could give them away. The whole circumstance was tense, but it was the tanned skin of their leader that wore the most lines as they viewed from afar.

With a *clink* of their hinges, the pub doors swung open and revealed a familiar face to the lads: Jack, the threatening beast they'd bumped into mere hours before. Although he had clearly been enjoying a beverage, or several, he had a swagger and air of nauseating confidence that hid the sins of alcohol from most passersby. Every sway just appeared to be part of who he was. Only a few steps away, the Manchester born and bred male felt completely safe and assured in his home city; the streets and establishments of the local area his to reign over. But that cocksure demeanor rapidly melted away when Kevin called out to him.

"Oi! Jack!"

Unperturbed, although a little surprised, Jack eyed the other with contempt, his lack of respect for the Londoner as clear as freshly fallen snow. "Fucking hell!" He boomed back. "Last I saw you I was sticking something in you and you were on the end of it!" Even though the mockery wasn't aimed at him, Justin felt its sting as his own, and that only proved to exasperate him further. This guy was a real piece of dirt, a kingpin to other wannabes, and the only way to derail his superiority was to show that he was nothing more than a babe in adult clothing, playing a part that was never meant for the likes of him. Although there were some comparisons that called out to Justin, he did his best to push them aside.

"Now it's payback!" Kevin wailed, the lads automatically jumping out on either side before the 'ck' had fully sounded from his voluptuous lips.

Despite all the talk and the swagger, the peacock display that was smoke and mirrors backed up by men to bolster his ranks, Jack stood no chance against the tide that raged and pulled him down on both sides. He tried, oh how he fought, but the hands and fists of men that felt slighted by him dragged him down to depths that only led to the hospital, possibly the morgue if Kevin had his way.

A ringing of rib after rib snapping like twigs sounded in quick succession that added a new tempo to an otherwise repetitive beat; *smack, kick, ouch, crack, snap*, on and on, each sound helping to break down Jack into an even smaller piece of his former self. He screamed out on several occasions, but a boot stamped down into his teeth each time, blood spurting out and dashing their toe ends and the pavement beneath, a marble effect starting to paint its way across the tarmac. It wasn't until that pattern spread in a radius from all angles that Kevin raised his hand to still their frenzy, the movement as hasty as their speed when they ran off in all directions, giggling with glee that their villain had been vanquished for good.

***

Much of the rest of the day followed a similar pattern, although they didn't target any one person quite as feverishly as they had dear Jack. Not that that took away their boldness and ardent spirits when they crashed like waves caught in an aggressive storm. What had started as a playful jolly with the odd rackus or two had turned into a free for all that they had always won, and always started; they were unstoppable. London legends who'd travelled from their home to spread the message that no one was untouchable, not even on their own turf. Something that they would have been best to have bared in mind when they rampaged through bar after bar.

A shower of wet glass rained down over their heads as Milton executed another bottling that grazed a man's whole face, not simply the crown of his head. It was brutal, it was beautiful, it was a twisted ballet that Justin knew the steps to like the palm of his hand.

***

Even though the shatter of bottles had been epically fun and exhilarating, it had been the finale of their brief time in that bar, for the owner had already been reaching and calling the police before glass had sprung forth all over the patrons. Still running on the fumes of their good times, the lads had decided to return to a familiar spot that they'd christened on their first day there. It hadn't taken long for another gang to get wind of their presence and poll on up ready to set the record straight that all London boys were pussies; *such a shame they didn't get the memo!* Justin jeered as he splintered the wood of the baseball bat they'd be concealing into the already marked face of a rival who was running low on how many of his features were left. The smash was like poetry in motion, and it sent a tinge of arousal down his spine, a sensation he would need to relieve by a different means when they hit the night scene later that night.

The girl he located this time was much like the last: harshly painted, skimpily dressed, and whispering in his ear how greatly she craved a man between her thighs. As a man who was on top of the world at the time, taking down names and fucking up the system of a well known criminal underworld, Justin had felt that he more than fitted the bill of what she wanted.

In the toilets, the grime scraping down her bare back with each slam of their bodies, Justin pulled nearly all the way out and then pounded back into her, their sex angry and rough. Her legs curled around his waist as she neared the end, his legs shaking from the strain of holding her weight, and because he was ready to pop like a bottle of champagne. With a stifled grunt accompanied by her pleasured whimper, their exchange was done and they both straightened up and went on their way. Before the night was through, Justin had set his sights on several other women who he imagined in positions similar to the one he'd just experienced. A few of them actually made it past the realms of fantasy.

***

On the very last day of their trip, the boys decided that taking it slow would only be an insult to all the hard graft they'd put in, and so they went out with the perfect bang: a face off against a group of footie fans outside one of the local football terraces. It hadn't lasted as long as some of their other brawls, but that hadn't taken away from the entertainment of it all. And while all of them rumbled with a relaxed kind of vigor, Justin had showed no signs of lessening his brutality; as far as he was concerned, a fight was a fight and it should always be done properly.

When they recalled how he had annihilated a guy with a chair to the back of the skull on the minibus ride home, all the cheers in the world couldn't remove that niggle of doubt that had been waiting in the wings to make an appearance once they had been headed for home. He didn't and couldn't deny how wild it had been, nor could he say that he hadn't savoured every encounter for varying reasons, but in the same breath he also couldn't say with complete honesty that it hadn't winded him. Jokes about learning from his dad were fine and dandy on a night out, but believing that was actually what and who he was burdened him greatly.

Chapter Fifteen

This part of the city just wasn't for him.

Justin tilted his head up and took in the monster size of the building, senses of amusement, jealousy, and discomfort all vying for prime position. This just wasn't a world he belonged in, and the fact that he looked so uncomfortable in turn caused him to look like a loitering thug preparing for a hit. In reality, he wished that was what he was doing, for it would have been a lot easier than the plan he actually had in mind.

Upon his return home the good vibes and ramped up moods took a nosedive into something that probably resembled holiday blues to most of society; he missed the drama, the blood pumping, the fever of being gripped by desires so primal you couldn't close your heart to them. However, he also missed normality, when he had been just another estate kid that, while he would never amount to much, didn't have the label of hoodlum teetering above his head. Neither of his parents had spoken of his reputation so he wasn't altogether sure whether they knew of it, but the way Danielle stared at him was enough to rouse suspicions. He wasn't so bothered about what his old man thought, but he did worry over how his mother would look at him. He just yearned for any facial expression over the ones that now faced him as he stepped into the reception area of the building he'd been surveying.

That cockiness he'd been carrying about all weekend dissipated in the line of fire of whirring fax machines, manic printing, and screaming telephones that shook and quaked when left unattended. As if the real world wasn't daunting enough, the sight of Eddie coming into view certainly was. Dressed in a crisp suit and a healthy glow that would fool anyone into thinking that someone else had been attacked, his sensible friend looked the picture of what life should be. It was only when Justin stepped closer that he noticed the sling that cracked the illusion from perfect to great, and reminded him that everything that had happened had been real. He couldn't keep wishing it away.

In that microsecond of being immersed in the normal everyday life of the modern man and his career, Justin had been consumed by fear and ready to stumble out of there, tail between his legs. But a tap from Eddie's colleague, who had caught sight of Justin and reasonably assumed that he was waiting for Ed, had ended his chance of running away from his problems. A pained look met Eddie's gaze, although there was no reflection of similar unease, instead he wore a smile alight with warmth and kindness towards Justin, a level of compassion he didn't merit.

Back on familiar ground, situated in a nearby park, Justin and Eddie occupied a time haggard spot on an old bench. They looked like their old selves, and in some respects they were, but some things just couldn't be undone, and that was to tarnish their relationship regardless of whether they could move forward or not.

"Married?" Justin asked in amazement.

"Yup."

"Bloody hell, what did you do!"

"Yeah, yeah, very funny." Came Eddie's second response, the banter between them sounding exactly as it had done before that alleyway stunt.

"Who is she?"

"A nurse." He stated, a twinkle of commitment dancing about his eyes. "Ironically I met her when I was brought into the hospital after the beating."

And there it was, the topic they'd flitted around until now, and of course it had to have been Eddie that had brought it up. In a bid to move on and forget that it had been mentioned, Justin lightly acknowledged the reference while strategically trying to shift away from it. "Fucking hell, really?" Although he knew, he just *knew* that Justin was skirting about the issue, Eddie danced to the tune and asked in kind.

"Yeah… if you can believe it." To which questions about whether she was nice and all the usual blah blah blahs were included; it was polite conversation that didn't suit them. Being friendly and interested in new life developments was one thing, but talking about it like two Victorian women in a drawing room wasn't. Another signifier of change. "So then, are you going to explain the look?" Justin looked up from the speck of dirt that had attracted him on the floor, a crinkle to his young brow revealing how unprepared he was for this section of their meeting.

Even though he was shaking on the inside, Justin had to be grateful where it was due, and Eddie was earning it by the bucketload. Ignoring the lack of time that had passed between them since the office and now, he was so happy that no verbal fights had broken out, even though he had expected them to come into play the moment he'd bid a 'hello' in the offices. At first he had thought that it was for his benefit, that his older mate simply didn't wish to draw recognition to a festering wound. But then after the chat about the woman, and the very location of their discussion, they all told him something else: that Eddie still cared deeply for him. The why behind it was something else. "What look?" was his delayed question, having been lost in a train of thought so chaotic that Latin appeared simple.

"Yeah, that hardman look and the look in your eyes."

"In my eyes?" *What is this crap? Just out with it already!*

"You look scared." Eddie remarked bluntly, unapologetic about how abrupt his commentary had been. And why should he be sorry for speaking the truth? Justin had been an utter idiot in a bid to be the adult he thought grown ups were, so what better way than to address him like said adult.

Deserved or not (and he guessed it was the former), there was no way he was going to take a comment like that from someone who didn't know him anymore. Scared? Him? He had just been tearing the city of Manchester a new one, and had fucked up many men and fucked loads of women that it seemed highly doubtful he would be scared of anything. Scared? What a load of- *truth. Fuck.* "Fuck off, I'm not!" was all he managed, the denial he was expelling not having caught up on the acceptance that sounded in his overworked brain.

"Ha. Yeah you are – you're frightened of yourself." Nail. Head. Hit. From there Justin spilled all the details of the road trip, not leaving a single detail out, determined to explain fully and in crisp detail exactly why he was having second thoughts about the path he was walking. Halfway through, while Justin was taking a breath, Eddie jumped in and stole the mic -

"Was this before or after you pissed on me?"

It was a shock that Justin hadn't been prepared for, to hear Eddie say aloud that he was aware the boy had urinated on him, it was more like a thunderbolt had shot down and welded him to the spot. His jaw tensed and his eyes bulged at the edges. For the life of him Eddie had no idea why this information was such a revelation to his troubled friend – he had seen Justin before the rest of the lads had kicked him unconscious, so it stood to reason that he would have been the one to seal the deal and brand him.

Not only was it logical, but Eddie had come from a gang just like theirs in his younger years, and so the ins and outs of how crews introduced you to the world of crime were widely known to him. If he had been some pompous stiff in a suit then maybe Justin would have gotten away with it, but despite what his appearance might have said to the outside world, he wasn't a man cut from that type of cloth. "I'm not a fucking idiot, I knew it was you." He added so that they were both perfectly clear.

"But I…"

"It. Was. You." Eddie sounded one word at a time, drawing them out and pronouncing them with clear definition.

"Then why didn't you say?"

"What? To the police?" He laughed openly in his face, struggling to belief that Justin had even asked such a stupid question. "What good would that have done? No, I kept quiet." Eddie threw a sideways look that didn't sit right on his features. "I may be a rich wanker, but I know the score."

The disbelief was unbearable and had no rival in which to compare it to – even when Kevin had played him and made Eddie the target of Justin's mark, he hadn't been so speechless. In the far fetched recesses of his overactive imagination, the fledgeling looked around from left to right, expecting to see a hundred coppers pop up like daisies and arrest him like they did in soap operas. They'd cart him away while he cried for mercy and forgiveness, finally seeing the error of his ways, meanwhile Eddie would retreat back to work and continue on with his life. The classic good triumphs over evil and wrongdoings, the homely message that eventually dominated one storyline or several. In some respects, he had wanted that to happen rather than *this*. "Why are you even speaking to me?"

"Don't get me wrong, Justin, I fucking hate you," a total lie on his part, but an emotion that was overriding all others in his present state. "You fucked me over and beat the shit out of me, and all just to impress your new friends. But for what, why?"

"Respect."

"Respect?! That's not what you gain when you do what you did. A man who works two jobs to put dinner on the table earns respect. A single mother who raises decent children in a rough neighbourhood, that's respect." Eddie now glared at him. "Loud mouth fucking idiots beating up people at a football game? Nobody respects that."

Justin couldn't allow himself to even glance in Eddie's general direction; he wasn't worthy and never would be. How stupid he'd been to think that hospitalising anyone was a quality that warranted praise, in what backward world had he thought he lived in? The answer was none. The reason was that it hadn't been about rationality and making sense, but about being anything other than himself. The estate had birthed him, but it hadn't *made* him, but fighting, fucking, and clawing his way to the top of the local dog pile would have changed that. Or that was the ideology he'd be working with, in practice it had worked out a lot differently.

Teenage daydreams and recklessness were all part of puberty and going through the motions, nevertheless, the way he'd expressed these acceptable norms had been extremes that had damaged and alienated him. It had removed him from himself and others he held dear, and had led him to the safety of a man he wasn't sure he even liked. When he totally thought about it and asked himself, he couldn't pinpoint a single reason why Kevin was such a big deal to him. He was just another nobody pretending to be somebody. "I'm, I'm sorry."

"Do you want to be like your old man?"

"What?" Like it even needed a 'what', he knew the question and felt strongly about the answer.

"Your dad. He was like you, living it large at the weekend, getting drunk and getting into fights. Then he gets married, settles down, and where does all that anger go, who does he turn it onto?" It was all just too close to home.

I'm not my dad, I'm not my dad, I'm not, I'm not, I'm not. "I'm not my father," Justin muttered, although he never turned his head back to look at Eddie while he said it.

"Not yet."

"Why are you helping?!" He squawked, finally submitting to all the tension and confusion, hurt, lies, and mistakes. To the truths about himself and his dad, to the facts that he was totally screwed. It was all too much! How could he run from a demon he'd lovingly nurtured and tended to? He was a victim of his own doings, and it terrified him. "Some friend I am." He added, pity jumping in as the temper simmered to a lukewarm splutter.

"Yeah." Eddie agreed, not able to lie no matter how badly he wanted to stop the hurt, and by god he wanted to help. Justin had been a fool, a moron even, but he'd been convinced by a mastermind of manipulation who preyed on the weak and moulded them into mini soldiers. This pitiful boy had been in the belly of the beast and yet was sat there today looking for a way to cut himself out and to freedom; some may have turned him away, washed their hands of him, but he couldn't. If the Justin he used to know was waiting to be rescued, he couldn't fail him because of what Jay had done in his place.

As his mouth opened and the words formed in his throat, Eddie questioned somewhere in the back of his mind why he was about to do this. "I have a friend in the IT department that needs an apprentice." Even after he'd finished saying it he couldn't comprehend why he had, there was helping and then there was giving handouts, and the latter of the two options wasn't something thugs deserved. *But he's not a thug*, he reasoned with himself as he read the reaction on Justin's deflated face. Thrown off by it all, he looked up and asked, rather reasonably, what the hell he knew about technology and computers. He could work his mobile, and laptops were something he'd played about with – hadn't all teens – but he wasn't a nerd. "You don't need to know anything, it's why it's called an apprenticeship."

"A job?" Again, he didn't get it.

"Yes… a job." Which was followed by a pleading but excited 'really', which meant that Eddie had to repeat the word 'yes' one more time; the repetition was irritating when it was so blindingly obvious what he was offering. "Be the better man." Eddie implored.

Maybe it was the tranquility of the park, or the fact they'd ironed out some if not all of their predicament, but Justin felt elated like he hadn't since he was a child. Back then toys had been the blueprints for the future, with wishes the fuel that turned playtime into anything being possible. The fact that he could recall those memories, even when so much darkness had shrouded them, made hope seem more than a crock of shit that hippies and self love enthusiasts threw at everything as an answer to world problems. Maybe, just maybe, he had a chance of being normal, of being someone more.

Chapter Sixteen

In another part of the municipality of London, with its fast lane lifestyles and questionable politics, sat Milton and Lloyd enjoying their space from the rest of the group after another weekend of debauchery. Although they missed the trouble that they managed to scare up when on the prowl, both men couldn't ignore how much they had missed having a quiet laugh and drink. When the numbers were reduced like this from six to two, it gave them a chance to discuss less turbulent affairs, such as their jobs, their screws, and reminisce about bits of Manchester that the likes of Kevin and his new pet Justin had missed out on.

Having been determined to have a few and then leave, the seasoned men still left in a stumbling, laughing huddle while their morning alarms prompted them through a series of notifications that they'd hate themselves in the morning. As sad as it was to call it a night, their stories of adventures past and present provided a suitable diversion while they placed one limp foot in front of the other, with home their destination. Their distractions, while good for them, soon turned on them when a *smash* from nearby failed to penetrate their drunken haze quick enough. By the time they were looking towards the noise, there stood a half battle worn Jack, his face still swollen from their unforgiving show back up north.

Even though that should have worried them given their mental state, and how fucked off Jack would be, Milton and Lloyd managed to poke and prod all the same, as if they were playing with a kitten and not a slumbering tiger. "Fucking hell." Started Milton.

"What brings a northern cunt like you down this way?" Lloyd finished in what was a respectable manner given that they'd tussled twice. To that Jack grinned, though it lacked any pleasantry or amusement, his eyes dead.

"I came to see what all the fuss is about in London."

"Yeah? What do you think?"

"Disappointing." Jack sneered. Meanwhile, from behind the duo a couple of men stepped from the shadows and grabbed them, the sudden violation nothing when collated against the caving in that the back of their heads took as they lulled forward.

***

The blackness that had rushed up with the ground was washed away by a bucket of ice water raining from above, the torrent and amount enough to cause them to choke as the water filled their unsuspecting throats. It was an unbearable way to be woken up, much like being hit in the stomach with a sledgehammer. While they vaguely remembered being struck from behind, and a conversation with Jack prior, they hadn't been expecting to wake up and find themselves moved and bound in place. As they looked down at their bodies, taking in the details of their imprisonment, Lloyd and Milton struggled against the ropes that criss-crossed all over their frame. It was bad, very bad, especially when Lloyd removed his gaze from the ropes to their surrounding environment: an abandoned warehouse lined with men.

In any other circumstance Lloyd would have laughed at how stereotypical it all was: the kidnapping, being tied up, the dank location nobody visited anymore, but when faced with the facts that he was the one on the receiving end, the situation lost its humour. This was the type of place where messages were made and sent, and that meant that the punishment they were about to be delivered would make their raid on Jack look like children running around with sticks for swords. The two of them couldn't take on this many even if they figured out how to break free and do a runner.

From in the depths of the shadows, as if to confirm their unfavourable fate, a low chuckle purred, filled with malice that they'd envy if they weren't about to feel its wrath. Bidding goodbye to the shroud of blackness he'd used for cover, Jack emerged from behind his row of men.

"What the fuck?"

"You fucking prick," Lloyd spat, wriggling around like a dying fish on a hook. "You realise you're dead meat don't you?!" Jack laughed again, right in his face, hearty and relaxed, as if he was watching his favourite television programme and not about to torment his hostages.

"We all die eventually, gobshite."

"Fucking hell." Milton breathed, any bravery he might had stored now dissipated; he admired that Lloyd was soldiering on, but he doubted he'd keep that up once the punches rolled in.

Jack couldn't help but keep grinning, the tear stretching from ear to ear, a joker like resemblance adding to the madness of his appearance. He was crazed, and he was looking for revenge. Kevin had been so consumed by it that he hadn't respected the unstated codes of conduct that governed them all; Kevin had cried like a baby and thrown a tantrum, disregarding the facts that doing something so dissent would be most unwise. What is more, while it wasn't that smart of him to return in kind, Jack couldn't just sit and watch the opportunity of making clear that he owned Kevin pass him by. "You both look scared." He cooed to them, his voice silky like a lover, making its effects all the more unnerving.

"Fuck you."

"Oh my, now that's a good comeback." He joked, turning to look at the men circling the room, all of them mimicking his face with their own.

"We will find you!" Lloyd roared. "We'll kill you!"

EMMA L. FLINT

"Oh," Jack breathed. "I know you will, well, you'll try at least."

With a nod of his head, two men singled themselves from the horde, evidently they were the guard dogs on duty ready to respond to the whims of their master. The new players and their zombie inspired state made Lloyd's body tighten, an action that Milton shared as they exchanged quick looks at one another; these boys were about to do the dirty work that Jack had been hinting at. And judging by their size and body mass, it was going to be as agonising as humanly possible. Both men prayed for unconsciousness to claim them quickly once the onslaught started.

The two men worked in unison, a timely dance of synchronised robots, and went on to hold Milton's legs steady as they undid the restraints, and although he tried to kick them away, their grip was too firm and instead pinned him into place. And that's when Jack reappeared with a baseball bat, one similar to the one both Justin and Kevin had used throughout their time in Manchester. "What the? Fuck off! Get the fuck OFF ME!" The aggressive chorus triggered Jack to twirl the bat around like a ribbon, his eyes so alight that they glowed amber.

"I like a good rumble, especially at a football match, but you know what sport I like-" He raised the bat high into the air, like a champion presenting his trophy. "Surgery."

"YOU FUCKING ASSHOLE! YOU FUCKING PRI-!" Milton poured out, his tirade of shouts cut unnaturally short by the swish and fall of Jack bringing the baseball bat down on both legs simultaneously. The scream that ripped through Milton's lungs and sliced at the air belonged in the land of movies, such was its power, the only sound more nauseating being the crunch of crumbling bones as his legs hung in half, bones protruding from mutilated flesh.

Keen to admire the mess he'd made Jack stepped back, and what he saw was the most glorious scene he could ever have imagined.

The way the bones flaked and spiked like snapped chalk, the blood and torn muscles clinging to the jagged marrow that was exposed. "That's the fucking stuff!" He bellowed, the pooling on the floor only furthering his delight.

"You… fucking… bastard…" Milton panted through gritted teeth, the pain not quite enough to cause him to pass out, but astonishing all the same. Feeling for his friend, and fearing for himself, Lloyd shot a smart remark to Jack.

"When the others find out, we're going to find you and they're going to—"

"They probably will," Jack interrupted, his grin now permanently stuck on. "And you can all have a good chuckle about it. You could even clap… if you were able to."

"What?" Was as far as Lloyd got before the men turned to him and treated him to the same hospitality as Milton, only this time it was his arms that bore the brunt of the assault.

Despite knowing that nothing would stop that awful baseball bat ripping his arms to shreds, Lloyd still fought against the taut pull of the men as they straightened his arms. The only blessing being that, while it was going to fucking hurt, both arms would suffer at the same time instead of one after the other, or that was what he had thought. But as the bat swung high and then rushed down, it was his left arm that snapped outward against the weight and force. His screams flooded the warehouse, assaulting the rusted walls and stained floors, and was soon followed by his begging as he watched the weapon ascend once again. Lloyd wasn't a coward, and he would always hold his own, but there was no way he wasn't going to plead to be left alone; survival was more important than pride right now.

The fall of the next break was so aggressive that his right arm virtually snapped in two, his wailing complementing the smashed bone and its multiple breaks. Which was when the bellows of all the Manchester crew, who had been watching silently up until now, joined in; it was quite the show. "You fucking cunt, you fucking cunt!" was being chanted by Lloyd now, his pleads having failed and so his last resort being abuse, but to what ends not even he knew.

"Yeah." Jack confirmed, unable to deny what he knew to be true. Then he looked to his men. "What do you think – do you think they got the message?" Lloyd and Milton watched and listened as they all laughed, thoroughly appreciating a joke that they would never be in on unless death took them in this bleak moment. "That's the problem isn't it? The message isn't for you. No, you need to deliver it." Jack reached into his jeans pocket and whipped out a knife, its metal twinkling in appreciation of being shown to the world.

"Personally."

Chapter Seventeen

The hospital the following day was a scene that Justin wouldn't easily forget, and it was a sight he felt responsible for. Although he hadn't been the only person behind Jack seeking vengeance, he had played a part that had inevitably lead to Milton and Lloyd being broken residence in this dismal place, husks of their usual selves. Before him was Lloyd, Milton still confined to intensive care, and on either side of him were the rest of the guys: Frankie, George, and Kevin.

They were all listening intently as their injured comrade regaled to them what had happened, no details spared although the very mention of the event caused Lloyd to tremble uncontrollably. "He meant business," He continued on, his voice wavering with each breath, a rattle from his chest drawing attention to the broken ribs he was nursing. "That you'd taken it too far, that going on his turf was a bad move." Suddenly he looked away from them all, his eyes clasped tightly shut, as if he was trying to delete the memories that kept replaying in front of him. "He said that's why me and Milton were getting it; we were the message."

"How's Milton?" George offered as a way to distract, but it proved no use.

In his own personal room laid Milton, his legs strung up in plaster casts, his face wrapped in padded bandages to soothe the deep cuts that hid underneath the folds. Anyone looking in or walking past would be forgiven for assuming he'd been in a car accident or similar. But they'd have been wrong. No, instead he'd been a victim of a gang war that Kevin had started simply because he wasn't able to keep his urges in check; it made Justin boil.

Though it sounded like he wasn't the only one.

"How the fuck do you think he is? They sliced his face and then pissed all over him!" Even though he had so much more to say, Kevin jumped in and rallied his troops.

"Don't worry, we'll get the fucking prick."

Justin nearly had to lift his jaw off the floor, such was his amazement at what had just been said. In a time like this, when the crew needed to regroup and admit defeat, however unpleasant, there Kevin was talking about taking the fight back to Jack and putting more of them at risk. It made absolutely no sense, they'd played and they had lost, it was better to just let this one go. Sharing his views, although he wasn't aware of them, Frankie questioned their leader openly. "What?"

"We're going to find him and we're going to fuck him up."

"Kevin," George intervened, also unable to stand by and listen to more disillusioned fighting talk. "He fucking beat us, he's serious."

"I'm fucking serious! He comes here and wants to try and fucking beat us? He is still going to be here and we can still…"

"He'll be waiting." Justin finally said, deciding that enough was enough.

Kevin looked at him with an expression that he couldn't place, but that he was sure was in between hate and anger, but he just didn't care anymore. Everything that Eddie had warned him about was coming true, and although he couldn't alter what had occurred, he could make sure he was no longer part of the life Kevin wanted to champion. Kevin went to ask what the hell he thought he was doing sticking his oar in, but Justin carried on. "That's the point of all this. He fucks us up, gets you all riled up and angry, and then you go gunning for him. That's what it's all about."

"A trap." Frankie stated plainly, just to make sure that their points were being heard, to which Justin nodded.

"Son of a bitch."

He thought, for a brief period, that he had made them all see that suicide was exactly what they'd be opting for if they charged in now after a message like this, but Kevin ruined all of that naivety as soon as he composed himself. "So fucking what?"

"What?" Justin shot back, hoping he'd misheard in some way however implausible that seemed.

"I said so fucking what! He walks away? Just like that? What about respect? Honour?"

"Fuck respect." George spoke for the group, all of them tired of chasing something that was getting them maimed and closer to death than they wanted to be at this point in their lives. It wasn't worth it if they wouldn't be alive to experience that respect for themselves. Shockingly, Kevin pushed himself right up to George, the 23 year old staring at his friend as if he was suddenly the enemy. It was a horrible turn of events that nobody needed right now, especially not in the company of Lloyd who was still reeling from last night.

Kevin didn't care though, and that was the problem that had been there all along.

"What you fucking say?" He gobbed into George's exposed face, all signs of them being brothers meaning nothing.

"He'll fucking ruin us, Kevin, it's not worth it." Came the pleading reply, the older of the two, although not by many years, was hoping that his age and how long he'd known Kevin counted for something at least. Sadly though, it meant nothing to him. *They* meant nothing to him.

"You fucking coward!"

Justin reached out his arm and grabbed Kevin's to still the fight that was about to spring forth and turn the hospital into a common bandit hive rather than a place of health and wellbeing; he wasn't going to let that happen. Not this time. This time he wasn't going to be the yes man that they'd been fashioning him into since the beginning. "Kevin, back off." He encouraged, though his voice was firm, unwilling to bend.

"Back off? I'm going to fucking find him…"

"Of course you'll fucking find him – you'll find him and he'll be waiting for you."

"Good, then we can show him how we do it in London. With fucking honour."

Finally, although it did little to relax Justin, Kevin stepped back from George, the object of his annoyance no longer his fellow gang member but the rivals back in their safety net of the north.

Although he didn't agree with him, Justin could understand why Kevin wanted to challenge Jack: he'd taken so much from Kevin already, not just a chunk from his arm, so the chance to completely end him was worth more than the discovery of gold in the Thames. It just wasn't worth it though, was it? Was risking your lives, the lives of your mates, what mattered when it came to gaining honour? Eddie's shaking head and disapproving face loomed in the fore of his mind to confirm what he knew.

"So what if it's a fucking trap? We'll walk into it and show them we don't take shit. You know why, you know how?" He waited but nobody answered, and so he rushed on. "We get all the London crews together. All of them. We find them and we fucking take them on."

"All of them?" Frankie quizzed, his accent thick with uncertainty about whether a feat was even possible.

"Every single one of them, we show those northern wankers what a fucking fight looks like."

How inspirational – you go and hand yourselves to the fuckers who have just totalled two of our guys. The urge to punch Kevin in his arrogant fat mouth was increasing on what felt like a second by second basis. Any gleen that had coated him once and made him almost godlike to Justin had just washed off and revealed nothing more than a piece of shit who craved violence. This wasn't about revenge or defending Milton and Lloyd, it was just an excuse to get into another battle.

And yet there Frankie was, nodding along like a bobblehead on the dashboard of a car. Worse were the words that uttered from his lips. "We could beat them then."

"I don't want to beat them." Kevin admitted, knowing that his veteran friends would know exactly what he meant by such a comment. "What do you say?"

"Fuck it." Laughed Frankie, in a turnaround that Justin was expecting to be the end of a well crafted joke, for if it was an honest change of heart, it was one of the most stupid he'd witnessed.

"George?"

"I don't like my life much anyways." He too laughed, and so their eyes fell onto Justin, with the words 'Jay' being formed by Kevin as he watched in unnerved awe. As if he needed any confirmation that the decision he had made was the correct one, Justin looked from the men to Lloyd to which his body sagged.

Was this it if he said yes, to know he'd be back in the hospital in a day or two in a state like this, or worse, in the morgue? It couldn't be all there was to life, to friendship. It was time to lay his cards on the table and accept his lumps. He turned away from George and Frankie, their expectant faces turning his stomach into knots. Looking Kevin dead in the eyes, his expression plain and unamused in spite of the smile that was looking back at him, Justin did what he should have done from the very beginning. "When does it stop?" At first Kevin shrugged and gave a look that seemed confused, but then when Justin didn't say anything more, the man gave up and asked what was meant by such a silly comment. "When will it stop?" He repeated.

"It stops when I say it stops." Kevin replied, his true colours finally showing through the costume of friendship he had worn so well.

"It stops for me."

In the time that Kevin stood transfixed to the spot, unable to move due to how gobsmacked he was at the nerve of Jay, after all he'd done, Justin gave a small nod to the others and then brushed past his once great leader – *was he ever?* – and headed to the door. "You don't walk away from me, Jay! Nobody walks away from me!" To which the freed boy turned back, internally ashamed at how crazy he'd been to believe any word that escaped from such a manipulative liar.

"You once said you'd never tell me what to do."

"Things change." Was his matter of fact reply, as if being economical with the truth was okay when it suited him. Well that wasn't okay for Jay… *Justin.* Aware that such tactics weren't going to work with the stubborn fool, Kevin opted to try and blackmail him to get the teen to stay. "I know what you did…" An admission Justin had been waiting for.

"So does Eddie." His ace in the hole. Before any one of the them could say anything further, to which he didn't have any intention of listening to after how dismissive they'd been of Milton and Lloyd, Justin stepped out of the room and into the cool air of the corridor. Although it had been a simple passage through a door, it had felt like a rebirth to him.

Chapter Eighteen

When he had left the hospital, while feeling powerful and in control, Justin had needed a sense of guidance back in his life. In a time before Kevin, when that name had been that of the black postman and not of a gang member, he had turned to Eddie for advice in every aspect of his life, seeing the man as a substitute for his dad. Now however, it felt awkward to put that pressure onto their drawn friendship. However well they'd managed to move on after their talk in the park, they were by no means the same, which meant he had two options: he could go home and deal alone, or he could talk to Danielle.

Positioned on a bench along the roads of the estate, Justin was sat close to Danielle, the fact that they were functioning just as they had done before all this was a comfort he couldn't fully express to her. While she had been an initial advice hotline, the topic had soon moved along to better things, to the fact that Justin had some promising news that showed him all too clearly that he could be a man made of respect that was earned through more than his fists.

"A job interview, really?" Danielle said aloud, the delight flushing her cheeks that attractive pink hue, as well as the undeniable pride that welled in her voice, making Justin go weak at the knees.

"Yeah." He blushed back, so pleased that she was impressed by his development.

"Wow, well done." After he rushed out a word of thanks, Danielle carried on, her words a little more carefully chosen. "Well, Jay, I am so glad—"

"Dani, please just call me Justin." He cut in, the very mention of his bully alterego making him struggle to hold back the bile that rose in his throat. It hadn't been that long since he'd waved bye to it all, that was true, but that hadn't stopped the mortification setting in when his foot had stepped outside the hospital.

Danielle beamed at him now, all sorts of questioning swimming in her eyes as she looked at the boy she had thought gone forever. It sounded too good to be true, and she suspected that it probably was, but for now she would savour every moment of Justin being returned to her. The man she loved, even if she wasn't about to tell him. "Really?" Before Justin was halfway through a nod, she sped on throwing caution to the wind, judging that the mood was good so little would spoil it. "Thank fuck because Jay was a stupid name." *Oh, Dani, you're too good to me, even if you're a bitch sometimes with your wit and sarcasm.* "I am glad though."

"Yeah, well, I thought it was about time I grew up…"

It was as good a reason as any, and she couldn't deny how badly he'd needed to grow into the manhood he'd be swanning around in since hitting the local pubs, but that wasn't the only reason why she was glad. "It's not about growing up, you know." Not that she expected Justin to understand, which it appeared that he didn't when he looked at her quizzingly. "It's about deciding who you're going to be for the rest of your life." That was the meaning of life to her at least, and even if it wasn't wholly correct, it was a worthy goal to work towards.

"I'll be honest, I don't think I have that part figured out just yet."

"Nobody does, Justin. Nobody wants you to join the rat race, you know, all they want is for you to be the good man we all know you can be."A sentiment that caused the pair to squeezes one another's hands in an exchange of feelings that were best left unsaid for the time being. As if they'd been right to avoid overly flamboyant displays of affection, Danielle mentioned that she needed to go, and so Justin whispered her a tender farewell and watched as she walked away, the sway of her hips catching his eye in a way they hadn't previously.

As mesmerising as her curves had been to him, they hadn't been able to stop him from noticing that Kevin was stood a little down the road in front of him. He didn't look thrilled that he had to witness what Justin had been reduced to, but he hoped that a good talking to would knock some sense into him… Well, that was one way to do it.

"So… you fancy the birds a bit plainer looking?" A quip, how ept of him to open with after the jerk he'd been at the hospital. Struggle though he did, Justin didn't raise to the ugly bait that had been dangled like a carrot in front of him.

"I'm going home."

"We're not finished yet." Came the curt answer, to which Justin had to ask why that was the case – did Kevin think he could talk his way out of what he'd done and how he'd behaved? Rather smugly, the friend he'd once shared a joint with revealed that they knew where Jack now was. "We found him, holed up in a grotty hotel."

Even though he had thought he didn't care, there he was fighting the urge to find out more about the location of his rival; not rival in a gangs sense any more, but one in sense of being an enemy for hurting his friends. Finally, and much to his annoyance, he caved and asked what he desperately needed to know – "Where is it?"

"It doesn't matter where, we know the old bill won't be up that way." That explained the confidence that Kevin had; without the police around, the London crews involved could play as dirty as they wanted without immediate repercussions.

"How many crews?"

"Four."

"It won't make a difference." Justin said sorrowfully.

"You're a fucking—"

"Do you know how Milton is, have you been to see him?" He threw back at him, uninterested in what he was and wasn't in

Kevin's opinion; he only cared whether the disgusting man was aware of his friend's wellbeing or not. That would be the last test of his character, and one Justin didn't expect that he would pass.

Kevin sniggered at this, baffled as to why it even mattered – Milton was out of the picture, he couldn't fight. Even if he had begged to join the rally, which he hadn't, he'd have been nothing but a liability in his condition and thus he'd risk everyone because of his stupidity. Kevin didn't need deadweights. "How the fuck should I know?! I've been too busy fucking arranging this." As if that was a good enough reason to neglect people who were meant to be friends.

"I saw him today," Justin made known, tired of their back and forth. "He's blind in one eye, and he's going back home to his mum and dad in Devon."

"Hooray for fucking Milton." Kevin mocked, yet another way to ensure that Justin's back was up like a cat faced with a drooling playful puppy. How he had never seen the coldness of his soul, the very essence of the monster he was, Justin wasn't sure – he wanted to say he'd never noticed it was there, but in truth he'd seen its ugly head plenty of times but had chosen to look the other way. It was easier to pretend not to see than admit that you did.

Not that it made this exchange any easier, in fact in some respects it made it a lot harder. More due to the concern Justin now had surrounding his judgement of character and whether he actually knew a person just because he hung out with them. People like Danielle and Eddie were different (he hoped), but what about the countless others he'd meet throughout his life, would they be as awful as Kevin had been? Although he wanted to console himself and say no, he was sure that there were just as many people milling about in the world that would be just as cruel, if not more so. "You don't care that Milton's leaving?" Justin forced himself to say, already mindful of what reply he'd get; Kevin rolled his eyes and flung his arms outward in an aggravated display.

"Milton? He took one for the fucking team, he's earned his rest."

"He didn't take one for the team, "Justin retaliated, repulsed that having your body mutilated and broken, not to mention urinated over, was classed as 'taking one for the team'. Something about that analogy, that sense of being maimed equalling respect was very wrong. "He got fucked over, and for what exactly?"

There hadn't been many moments in his life when he'd stood aghast because of someone else, but this was one of those rare occurrences. Here stood some jumped up idiot, a sack of shit that had come from nothing, and was headed to nowhere fast, and what had Kevin done – he'd taken him under his wing. Potential was there, and if it was developed correctly the newbie could become a valuable asset, aka weapon, for the gang. *Ha, so much for that!* He scowled, annoyed that he'd been fooled by someone; it was meant to be the other way round. Where had Justin's balls disappeared to over the days? He'd started out as eager to please, not openly seeking approval but yearning for it all the same, and then he'd beaten up Eddie and the reality of life had gotten the better of him. What a piss poor ending to something that should have worked out beautifully.

If Justin hadn't been hell bent on shoving a stick up his backside, Kevin was positive that they'd have taken down Jack with effortless ease that would have been talked about for ages. They'd be legends. *Ah well, guess I have to be a legend all by myself.* "You're a fucking idiot." He fired off, expecting the boy to maybe fall at the last hurdle and admit that he preferred praise over dismissal. But Justin didn't budge for he knew what was right and what was wrong, even if it had taken him a while to uncover it.

"I'm done, Kevin."

"You're done when I say you're done. We're going there Friday and *you're* coming with me." Even though there was menace there, all the other did was shake his head in a firm and defiant 'no'; it wasn't going to happen. It was that simple to him, yet to the older of the two, it was unthinkable. "*Yes you fucking are.*"

"Come on then." Justin had had enough of this crap – they'd have to fight it out and then just walk away. If that was the only language Kevin spoke then that was how he'd have to tackle this one.

Ready or not, Justin hesitated to throw a punch, which allowed Kevin to seize his opportunity and crack the teenager straight on the nose, a *crunch* but not a break echoing between their now entangled bodies. All the tension, all the enmity, every drop of fear, confusion, and doubt came to a sticky film on the surface, a murky smear on a relationship that had always been toxic. How they'd ever thought working together would have worked out long term was a thought that vaguely exploded with each hit of a limb.

Although Justin was fired up the way he always was during a tussle, he didn't need to be an outsider watching to be aware how badly he was doing; Kevin had the upper hand, a factor he knew because every swipe became more threatening and wicked. Fists laced with poisonous desires and words flied back and forth like a turbulent dance, a piece of choreography that had favoured devout evil over the redeemer.

An almighty headbutt recoiled off of Justin before he sank down to meet the earth, his predator looming over him wearing the wickedness he always carried around with him. Spittle sprayed over him as Kevin arched his back and laughed out loud, a low deep laugh that wheezed through the pants of rawness in his throat. "Well, that was disappointedly fucking easy." He gobbed before leaning toward Justin's upturned red caked face. "Fucking. Loser." Followed by another snigger before he swaggered away like the hardman he thought he was, and in that moment that assumption felt affirmed by how easily Justin had gone down – like a stack of cards. Not that Justin cared, oh no, he smiled, ignoring the blood dripping into the grooves between his teeth.

Chapter Nineteen

Friday had always been a day of the week that they'd relished: it was a time of play, of mayhem and sex, where they could be the kings they convinced themselves they were and not the paupers they disguised themselves as all week. It heralded in a two day window of opportunity, giving them 48 perfect hours to live free of responsibility and its repercussions. They'd lived for the weekend. They *were* the weekend.

This weekend eve though was divergent.

Outside a rundown hotel that barely looked capable of standing, crouched George, Frankie and their kingpin, Kevin, their eyes darting from one window to the other, trying to make sure that they couldn't be seen from this vantage point. If they had been seen, they'd have been marked as criminals just by how they were stood, let alone the place they currently occupied. But as luck would have it, no sane people ever visited this backwater slum. It was essentially London's missing link, that cousin that everybody just pretended never existed – 'what family member?' they'd ask.

Despite his eyes on the prize, his yummy treat being that of Jack and his soon to be corpse, Kevin was multitasking on his mobile, the other two acting as backup just in case. Even though they couldn't hear what was being exchanged between Kevin and the faceless voice, they judged it bad given how fuming their friend was. "What do you mean you aren't fucking coming? You fucking cowardly bastards!" Without speaking a word, Frankie looked to George with dread evident in his dry eyes; if the other crews were pulling out if was because they saw this as a bad idea. And bad ideas could lead to them looking like Milton and Lloyd. Frankie shuddered at the thought.

When the phone went dead, George asked what him and Frankie were both wondering. "They're not coming?"

"No." Kevin responded bluntly, his teeth gritted and his jaw clenched, a little muscle throbbing rapidly at the pressure it was withstanding.

"It's just us?"

"Yes, yes, it's just us alright (!)" What was with their questions? It didn't fucking matter, they'd tear Jack apart like a pack of hungry wolves.

"Well, it was a nice idea, but I think it's time we gave this up." George admitted, his own morality overriding the sensation of needing to defend his fallen friends. Right now he didn't care about them, they weren't here, and neither should he be.

While Frankie had agreed with the words he'd just heard, and he was grateful he hadn't been the one that had had to draw attention to the hopelessness of the plan, he couldn't help but cower slightly as Kevin burned at them. "You're fucking idiots aren't you? So much for your fucking honour!" He started to rise up, his head swaying violently like he was having a type of mental breakdown. "SO MUCH FOR YOUR FUCKING RESPECT!" And with that he pulled the knife he'd been protecting in his jacket pocket and started to make his way forward to the point of no return, where at least he would be crowned a hero. "Fuck it." Was his mantra as he cracked open the front entrance and disappeared inside, leaving George and Frankie to hightail it out of there. A decision that would prove most wise in the near future.

Inside it was the shithole he'd expected it to be, damp patches and musk the perfume of the downright lowliest of scum that holed up in there, scoundrels like himself. Normally that way of thinking would have brought a grin to his face, but the time for laughter and joking had passed, especially now that he was the only one that could do this.

The bored receptionist that was slumped behind the desk, the bags under her eyes as heavy as the bowed ceilings, didn't even so much as glance his way when he walked in and started to take in his surroundings. She didn't care who he was, he could be there to kill her and it wouldn't have mattered, in fact it would have been a lovely bonus to what had been a poor existence. Although it didn't matter to him one way or the other whether she looked at him or not, he loathed her attitude all the same. But she held the keys to Jack's kingdom, so he couldn't just knock her out and be done with it.

Forcing himself to play nice, Kevin growled at her for the room number he seeked, the roughness of his tones unintentional. Luckily for him, she hadn't cared how he'd spoken to her – she was used to being a dog to all the customers that waltzed on in through the door acting like they were important when actually nobody would even notice their disappearance. "Room 401." Came her deadpan voice, her vocal chords as bored as she was.

He muttered under his breath an attempt at gratitude but he had no clue whether it had reached her ears or not, and right now she could go fuck herself if she had taken issue with that fact. Kevin was on a mission, and that mission was at the end of the corridor he was stomping down, his feet like lead shoes on hardwood flooring; stealth wasn't his strong point, and Jack didn't deserve it. That man needed a full on frontal assault that was loud and brash, like his cockiness had been when he'd targeted Kevin and made an example of him, twice. And that's what it had been with Lloyd and that sorry sack of shit Milton: it had been about him. Kevin. He was the one that Jack had gunned for, that he had called out and made a fool of. Fuck Justin and his sympathies for they were misplaced.

Lost in thought as he had been, he didn't fail to see the bold '401' smacking him in the face in spite of its lacklustre sheen that had faded with age and lack of care. *This is it, that fucker is gonna get what he fucking deserves. Cunt.* His fist hammered against the wooden door, the structure wobbly under duress. Nothing, no sound, no movement, no anything. Offering a little shrug to himself, Kevin continued and pounded on the door again, sure that this time Jack would at least breath funny to reveal that he was inside. But yet again, only quiet followed. Certain that he was being messed about, toyed with, he lifted his leg and caved in the door with a single blow, the smarting tips of his toes failing to even register when he looked upon the scene before him.

On the floor, cold and rigid lay Jack, his eyes glossed over balls of white and black, the life that once plagued him no longer there for anyone to see. Shocked though he was, it didn't take him long to locate how the death had happened, for a clean slit across the width of his throat informed him of all he needed to know. The bombshell that was wide eyed on the ground was now what scared him.

A flicker from out the corner of his eyes caused Kevin to drop his knife, the instinct to defend being taken over by undiluted fear; emerged from the shadows after observing the confusion was a well dressed man in a black suit, his face sombre.

"What the fuck happened?" Kevin enquired, despite the overwhelming warning in his head that was screaming that he should run while he still could. To this the man frowned.

"You were both making too much noise, Kev."

"What noise?" His head was overflowing with screams now, all of them them pointing and stating that the man in the room, the one so casual in his actions, was the one that would prove lethal if he stayed.

"I have business interests, and he was getting in the way of them."

"I don't give a fuck about your business interests!" *Kevin, man, we should. Go, go now.* The suit sighed with such feeling that it sounded like he despaired at how callous Kevin was with his life.

"You should."

His heart punched at his chest such was its alarm, but still Kevin remained rooted to the spot, his boldness pure and immovable, and most importantly, dumb. He was being stupid staying there when the writing was on the walls and in Jack's neat line of blood wrapped around his neck. "Listen you fucking old man…"

"Can you hear that?" The man interrupted, his head tilted as if straining to listen.

"Hear what?" *Cunt.*

"Exactly." He smiled without feeling, his word like the tip of a knife before it plunged in deep and severed every artery in its path. "Nobody will mourn you when you die."

"Mourn?"

A nod was the simple reply, though behind something more was stirring: another that Kevin hadn't been aware of, his heart having tricked him, unintentionally, to maintain focus on the man before him. The turn that he was halfway through executing was pointless for a blade quickly retracted from his soft flesh and back into the the jacket of the man he had half seen. The stabbing itself hadn't hurt, mainly because he had been too engrossed in being caught off guard that the serrated edge had gone in and out with no resistance. Now however, now it stung with a fury he'd only felt when fighting.

Kevin dropped to his knees, his mouth opening and closing in a desperate scramble for air, anything to keep himself from panicking now – if he remained calm he could get out of there alive. This didn't have to be the end for him. It didn't. Amused by how valiantly he was fighting, even now when fate was sending it's final message, the suited man looked down at the filth he'd once thought capable of anything. "I have business interests, and for a time your activities took attention away from them. The arrangement worked." He sighed sadly. "But then you had to go to fucking Manchester." As he stepped over the grasping man, the employer Kevin had boasted about to Justin had one last parting gift to instill. "This is a last lesson for you: you're not as important as you think you are." And the door swung shut, leaving Kevin to fumble in the darkness.

Unable to move such was the pain, he stumbled upon Jack's body, his eyes growing tired with approaching death beginning to glaze over as they stared at the ceiling, blood dribbling from the corners of his mouth. This wasn't how it was meant to end for him, he was meant to go further than this, and yet it was a finality he couldn't avoid; death came for him there in that hotel, with Jack his deceased guide.

Chapter Twenty

When morning broke, a time of day that had normally been for rich wankers and not him, Justin had stood in his room ready for the day. After several anxious looks in his full length mirror, Justin had breathed in deeply and reminded himself that today was the start of something new. All the shit that had followed him around and nearly destroyed him was gone now, and he could move forward with his life. He was a new man, and this was his new job, a gateway into a better life for himself and the family he hoped to have some day.

***

What a great first day – I think I did well, everyone seemed friendly, and I haven't got fired yet, was the sound of his internal monologue as he walked through the estate towards home. Nothing could dull his shine today, not even the flowers that were outside the house just a few feet away from him, Kevin's face staring out from a picture taken before his death. He wasn't without feeling, he knew that his ex friend had paid the biggest price of all to be the man he'd always longed to be, but he couldn't give the man another moment of his life. Not even in his death. Thankfully, as if angels had sent her to intervene thoughts that were regressing into a darker place, Danielle walked up to him. Her eyes roamed over his body, taking in his suit and tie and general polished looks. "Well look at you, aren't you looking handsome."

"Cheers, you're not looking so bad yourself." He winked, falling into step with her as they walked side by side past the stain of his recent history.

"What do you fancy doing tonight, the pub?" *Ah...* Justin wavered mentally as he heard the phrase 'pub'. Ever since his weekend blowouts, pubs had marked a beginning to a destructive end, and while they wouldn't always be that symbol, for the time being he wanted to avoid them.

Danielle lightly prodded him for a response. "Erm, I don't know, I was thinking about something else, maybe the cinema?" He suggested, for reasons that weren't solely fixated on his past: the cinema was much more date like, a notion that he was sure Danielle would note. And sure enough she did, much to his delight.

"Really?"

"Yeah. Get off home and I'll text you about it later, sound good?" She grinned before nodding and waving him goodbye, a spring in her step that wouldn't leave her for the rest of the day. Since school it had only been about Justin, no other boys had come close, and now, after so much time, he was finally in her sights for real. If she had looked back to see Justin's reaction, she would have noticed that he too had a lighter step since talking with her.

The rest of the walk home while not as interesting, definitely was pleasant enough, the sun proving an adequate replacement for Danielle. Once inside home, Justin called out to his mum to let her know that he was home, both to relieve any worries she'd been storing away all day, but also because he wanted to talk to her about his job.

His heart sank a little though when he went into the living room and spotted the empty bottle of drink stood proudly on the coffee table; his mother noted his glance but ignored it and instead welcomed her son home. Her clever boy was doing so well for himself lately, and she couldn't be prouder for it was clear that he was destined for good things, not like her and her deranged husband. "You're looking so smart, Justin." She said to him, her whole body glowing with unspeakable pride, an aura which Justin could feel from the doorway across the room.

"Thanks, mum. Do you want a cup of tea?"

"Go on then." She replied, her smile never waning as she rose out of her chair and waddled into the kitchen in hot pursuit of her son.

When they both reached the kitchen, Justin dutifully started to reach for all the components he needed to make his mum a drink, the two of them intending to sit down and chat about the new job, maybe even Danielle if he felt brave. Now seated beside his mother, blowing on a steaming cup of Yorkshire based blend, Justin started on about his day. "It's a good job, a really good job." He concluded, wanting more than anything to assure her that the nuisance he'd been over the last few months was a man she would never have to see again.

"I'm glad, sweetheart, I'm so glad you're enjoying it." Justin revealed a brilliant grin as he swelled with fulfilment for the first time in his life. Never before had he ever felt like he'd accomplished anything worthy of note, and yet here he was finally doing it.

With a steady breath in, Justin carried on to what went hand in hand with him moving forward with his career: getting away from the estate and starting a new, preferably with his mother in tow. "I don't want to stay on this estate, mum; I want to be someone and make something of myself." Although he knew there was no need, he felt like he should apologise for saying this to her after she'd spent 18 plus years raising him while an abusive husband used her as a slave and target practice. His mum wasn't offended though, and for that he was thankful.

"I know, darling, and you will."

"Maybe I can try and help you…?" He started to say, though the soft shake of her head told him all he needed to know – as far as she was concerned, her time had passed and it was now down to him to go forward. "Mum… we can't all stay here."

"Don't worry about me, just get yourself out." The words struck him harder than he'd have liked, despite him knowing deep down that she was right in what she was saying.

In the cold harsh light of day, when he looked at it with clinical eyes, it was blindingly obvious that they both couldn't leave. If his mum was to attempt a coup it would just poke the sleeping dragon that was his father, and if he stayed he was positive he would end up killing the man in a crime of passion for having had to witness, yet again, his mother sprawled on the floor. People like Kevin had been meant for the ground, not his mum.

"Maybe you can go out with that nice girl." Sounded his mum out of nowhere, shaking Justin from his thoughts momentarily.

"Dani? Mum, we're just friends."

"Oh dear, there's no such thing as just friends." Came her gentle trill back, Justin meeting his mother's chuckle with his own laughter as they sat and joked. Touched by how warm her son appeared, her withering hand reached out and carefully stroked his soft, youthful cheeks.

"You are a good lad, aren't you?"

Am I? Justin asked, but only himself, not wanting to upset his mum by seeming disrespectful to her thoughts and feelings. He had never been a boy that was black and white about the world, but instead believed that there was much grey that people too often tried to overlook to make their points heard. People weren't good or bad, they just did things that fitted into categories related to wholesomeness and wickedness, Bible believer or not. But after everything that had happened, after the destruction he had seen and been a part of, he wasn't sure whether he could (or should) be graced with the term 'good'.

Still, for the sake of an easy afternoon with his mum, not one of debate and questions, Justin offered up a false ray of hope by raising the corners of his lips and responded to her in a roundabout way,

never once saying a definite yes. "I try to be, mum. I try to be."
And that was true enough.

"It's never easy, not in the area we live in."

"I suppose." Justin muttered, not ready for this kind of
conversation.

"Not in the world we live in."

"We'll get out one day, mum, I promise." Was all he had to give
right now, but it was a promise he intended to keep, by any means
necessary.

"If only I could believe you."

BANG! Went the front door, his mum having jumped several
feet off her chair with utter terror; his dad was home, and if he had
judged the slam of the door and the bottle correctly, a storm had
blown in their way. But he was there though, and he could protect
his mum. Nevertheless, when his dad rocked in the doorway to
the kitchen looking like he would keel over from the sheer volume
of alcohol swimming throughout his body, Justin felt that maybe
he wasn't the knight she needed. What his mum needed was
nothing short of a miracle.

Even though he was sloshed to the heavens, undoubtedly seeing
birds and angels circle above his head, Justin's dad still managed
to look at his son and ask him why he was wearing a suit, his first
assumption being that he'd been in court for some reason. Whilst
he knew that it was a somewhat well placed guess, it bothered
him that his father had the nerve to associate Justin and the legal
system in the same sentence. Hell, even if he hadn't have had
work, he could have simply just wanted to wear a suit, it wasn't
like that would have been a crime. "Dad, I've been at work." He
rudely said, his nose upturned like he was sniffing the remains of
someone's faeces.

"Yeah right!" He chuckled before he staggered further into the
kitchen, making sure the smell of a thousand breweries tickled
and whaffed at their noses. *You utter bastard. Just die already and*

make us happy. Oh, and now he's gone to get more beer, are you fucking kidding me?! But sadly, the appearance of the bottle and its smoking top told him that his eyes had been truthful if not kind.

His mum, probably unwisely given the state her husband was in, tried to defend her son by stating matter of factly that their only child had been hard at work as an apprentice. What she hadn't added was that her son was actually worth something while he was nothing more than a lazy bum with no life to speak of other than his drink. Upon listening to his wife, Justin's dad delivered a gem of a line that, if spoken by a group of mates to their friend, Justin would have taken differently. "An apprentice cunt more like. There's no fucking point you know, it won't fucking work." His father added.

"I have to try."

"Yeah, you just try alright, you fucking prick." Spewed out his dad, his words venom like the liquor he constantly consumed.

"Justin, please leave the kitchen." A tense voice asked, the happiness she'd felt earlier gone and replaced by concern for keeping damage to a minimum, and by that she meant herself. She would bear the brunt of this rage, not her son.

Justin admired his mum for trying, but he didn't want to leave her with that man; he was so loaded up and already picking fights that it wouldn't be long until her cries floated up to his bedroom. And even a night out with Danielle wouldn't erase those whimpers and pleas as she took her lumps. "Please…" She implored further.

"Why does he have to walk away? Fucking wanker thinks he's fucking better than us?!"

"Fuck you." He retorted, his breaking point exceeded but not completely in tatters.

"What did you just say?!"

"I. Said. Fuck. You." Justin spelled out, not caring whether his dad went for him or not, in fact, he actually wanted him to challenge him. The man had it coming, and he wanted to be the guy that delivered it, fuck being family and all romantic notions of love and bonds, when it came down to it family meant nothing.

As automatic as his retaliation had been, Justin stood up and faced off to his dad, his father grinning a lopsided smirk that was begging to be smacked away into the gutter like his old man. Before he could do more than just glare, a sharp right hander blazed on his exposed cheek, a *thump* which had pushed Justin onto the floor, and in turn had caused his mother's screams to rip through the air and around the kitchen. The sound was more painful than the mark that started to grow there.

Although his dad had been drinking, his reflexes appeared to be quick enough to drag off Justin's work jacket, the fabric only having resisted for a moment before it allowed itself to fray and tear. Spurred on by anger, the injured teenage tried to stand and pull the garment back, but he was met by a well timed stamp that knocked him down again, the shock that rocked his core unsettlingly close to how he had felt when Kevin had placed Justin in a similar position.

Brave though it was, Justin's mother made the mistake to intervene, which landed her on the ground next to her son, the two of them forced to watch as the drunken beast that raged before them threw down the jacket, unzipped his trousers, and pissed all over the once pristine item. Although it had only been an outfit, an unimportant part of his life that he would be able to fix with little cost, it had still pained him to watch his dad do it. "I fucking know you, son, I know exactly what you've been doing and whom you've been doing it with, boy." Partially invaded his eardrums as he focused on the stream of urine coming from his father. It wasn't the jacket that hurt, but the act itself: his dad was marking him, just as he'd marked Eddie, the fact that Justin had been replaced by a jacket instead was but a minor detail. "You've been doing what kids have been doing on this estate for generations, just like me." He stated as he picked up the sodden and soiled attire and threw it on top of Justin's mother, her whimper muffled as the jacket covered her face. "You're just like me, boy."

Having started to return his genitals to their boxers, the man who Justin hated to call father had failed to notice him get up and walk behind him, his step careful and light, even though he hadn't tried. Fuelled by years of mental and physical abuse, of watching his mother time and time again conceal scars and hide away, Justin reacted and kicked his dad's legs from under him. "You fucking…" Was as far as his dad got before Justin shoved the nearest object he had grabbed into his father's face, the *crack* followed by another and another as the boy brought down the rolling pin in an unforgiving shower. Although he had quaked, had felt his legs lose their firmness, he had continued on, the form of his dad getting squishier and bloodier with every blow.

"Turn into you?! I'D RATHER BE DEAD!"

It was only when his mother's screams pierced the air that his own wailing escaped his throat to join them.

Epilogue

The cold grey wasn't as oppressive as he'd expected, and in fact he'd grown used to it before he'd even seen himself carted away to this garbage refuse of criminal filth. Maybe it was because he had always known that he had been headed here, that everything he had told himself that said otherwise had been nothing more than idle fantasies of council estate scum that had now gotten what he deserved.

We all choose options in life, he thought as he scrutinised the cracks in the wall, *some of us choose the basic package – we get a job, find a girl, settle down with kids in your newly bought house. Others however, choose a very different package and do whatever they want, constantly moving an unknown finishing line.* His dried hand reached out and touched the dents he'd been taking the time to sketch in his mind for the last several days, or was it weeks? He couldn't tell. *Eddie, bless him, he'd always wanted best for me, for me to do the right thing. Well, I've done that. Question is, did I opt for the basic package? Fuck no, I AM HOOLIGAN.* And for what had been awhile, too long in fact, Justin grinned with genuine conviction.

He was a thug, a hooligan, and it was fucking worth it.

Lightning Source UK Ltd.
Milton Keynes UK
UKOW02f2322250916

283805UK00001B/12/P